THE DEMON MASKS

THE 72 DEMONS
BOOK THREE

JAMES E. WISHER

SAND HILL PUBLISHING

CHAPTER ONE

The French countryside consisted mainly of rolling hills covered in lush green grass for the many cows and sheep to munch on. Helena found her drive through it peaceful despite knowing what was waiting for her at the end. The Pilat family lived about fifty miles north of Paris in a little town called Rostwel. At least that was what the ID they found in Julian Pilat's wallet said. She would've liked more information, but the unfortunate fellow was long dead by the time she and the others found his grave in the Australian outback. How he came to be there and have a demon seal in his possession were two of the many things Helena hoped to learn from his surviving relatives.

She'd done some unpleasant tasks during her handful of years working for the Circle of Sorcery, but delivering the news that someone's son was dead didn't number among them. And that was okay with her. During the short flight from Zurich and then the drive north, her mind had wandered from one thing to the next, basically anything to avoid thinking about what she was going to say to whoever opened the door when she knocked.

The dirt road came to an intersection and she stopped. She'd only met two cars since leaving the pavement ten miles ago. To say this part of the country was sparsely populated would be generous. The map on her phone indicated a right-hand turn and she made it.

That was the last turn before Rostwel. Fifteen more minutes and she'd have to face the task ahead of her.

How would Daisuke handle it? She smiled when she thought about him. Her handsome half-Japanese lover was the most powerful wizard in the Circle and a good man. If he'd been given this task he probably would have just said what needed to be said without batting an eye. Despite having a good heart, he could also be blunt to the point of harshness.

What was he doing right now? The thought had barely formed when an image of Jinx appeared in her mind. The beautiful Shadowen sorcerer was Helena's rival for Daisuke's affection. And what a rival she was. Helena had never seen a woman so stunning. Being a half demon no doubt accounted for some of it.

She thought of them as rivals, but Daisuke had made it clear that he had no intention of choosing between them and settling down into anything resembling a committed relationship. Given the dangers they faced on a regular basis, that was probably the wise decision, but she couldn't help loving him.

Why did things always have to be so complicated?

No voice from the heavens felt the need to comment. In the grand scheme of things, her relationship issues hardly warranted heaven's direct interest.

Ahead of her, the first house appeared. It was nothing special, just an old farmhouse made from stone, with a cedar shingle roof and windows that looked like they'd let in awful drafts in the winter.

She drove past a couple more outlying houses before eventually reaching the town proper. It had an almost medieval feel to it. Not surprising given how much the population declined after the war. A couple of battered pickups were parked in front of what she assumed was a bar or maybe a general store. Helena didn't know and wasn't overly interested in any case.

Leaving the town center behind, she started paying closer attention to the brass number plates on the houses. A quarter mile later she reached a driveway marked by a post engraved with the correct number. The path led to a big wooden farmhouse that she suspected had to be haunted. It was badly in need of a fresh coat of paint and some replacement shingles. One of the shutters was flapping in the breeze.

Helena had fought werewolves, demons, and pretty much anything else you could imagine, but she still got a chill looking at the farmhouse. Not that a little psychic chill was going to stop her from completing her task, but it did strike her as a bad omen.

She turned off the road and eased up the driveway. Her little compact two-door didn't have much clearance, so she was careful not to bottom out. By some minor miracle she reached the front of the house and parked. The place looked abandoned, but there was a fair-sized barn about thirty paces away. The owner's car might be inside out of sight.

Enough speculating. She switched the car off and set the parking brake. It went all the way to the floor and she doubted it was holding much. Still, the grade wasn't that steep so hopefully the car wouldn't roll away on her. She should've sprung for something fancier; it was the Circle's money she was spending after all.

A set of partially overgrown paving stones led to the front steps. Helena climbed them gently lest her foot go through the spongy wood. The bronze knocker gave a deep bong when she slammed it down.

Please let there be someone here that could talk to her. She really didn't want to go back with nothing to show for her time.

She could just hear faint steps before the door opened revealing a wizened woman of indeterminate years but who looked old enough to be Helena's grandmother.

"Madame Pilat?" she asked in French.

The old woman's eyes widened a bit but she nodded.

"My name is Helena and I have some bad news about Julian."

"He's dead, isn't he?" Mrs. Pilat asked. At least it was phrased as a question. She spoke with such certainty that Helena couldn't help wondering if she was some sort of psychic.

"I'm afraid so. Would it be possible for us to talk inside? I'm sure you're curious about what happened and there are a few things I was hoping you could help me understand as well."

"I knew he was." She made no move to invite Helena inside. "When my boy didn't come home, I knew there was only one possible explanation. Forgive me. Please come in. I'll put on a pot of tea and we can talk."

"I'd like that, madame, thank you."

Mrs. Pilat led her into the house. The interior wasn't in much better shape than the outside. The entry hall had nothing in the way of decorations and the carpet was worn so thin she could see the backing. A right-hand turn brought them to a small dining room connected to an open kitchen. A gas stove and refrigerator were the only appliances.

"Have a seat, young lady. I'll just be a moment."

Mrs. Pilat went into the kitchen leaving Helena to study the rickety table and chairs with a dubious eye. It would be rude to keep standing there and Helena didn't weigh that much. She eased into the sturdiest chair. It creaked, but didn't flex or collapse. So far so good.

In the kitchen Mrs. Pilat had a kettle on the stove. Unlike Daisuke, Helena quite enjoyed tea. It was one of the things she had in common with Jinx. Under different circumstances she suspected she and the half demon might have been friends. Maybe it was foolish, but she couldn't make herself like someone she thought of as a rival.

"It'll take a few minutes," Mrs. Pilat said. "I'd offer you a snack, but I'm fresh out of goodies."

"That's okay, thank you. Um, do you live alone out here?"

"Yes, it was just Julian and me after his father died. Now it's only me." She gave a sad shake of her head. "I'll live out my days here, the few I have left. With my boy gone, I doubt there will be many. Forgive me, I didn't mean to get maudlin on you."

"You have every right considering the news I brought. I was hoping you might be able to tell me a little about Julian. If it's not too painful."

"Not at all. There are few things I like talking about more. But first, may I ask you a question?" Helena nodded and Mrs. Pilat said, "Where did you find him? The last I heard, he was headed for Paris and a new job."

"My companions and I found his grave in the Australian

outback, hundreds of miles from anything resembling civilization."

"Australia! Good heavens, what in the world was he doing so far away?"

"That's one of the things I'm trying to figure out."

The tea kettle whistled, bringing a temporary pause to their conversation. Mrs. Pilat hurried back and poured the water into two cups and brought them over. She set one in front of Helena and settled in the chair across from her.

While the tea bags steeped Helena asked, "What sort of job was he starting?"

"I'm not exactly sure, but he was excited. He said it was a chance for adventure." She let out a wistful sigh. "Julian didn't especially enjoy the quiet country life. When he wasn't working, he spent most of his time online looking for a way out of here. He had a basic education of course, but no college and no skills to speak of. But he was a good boy and a hard worker."

Helena nodded as some of the picture became clearer. A bored young man looking for adventure would make a useful pawn for someone hunting dangerous relics. If he succeeded, great. If he died, no big loss.

She took her tea bag out and had a sip. Not bad, but it needed sugar. There was none on the table and her hostess showed no sign of offering any.

"How did you happen to be in Australia?" Mrs. Pilat asked. "They don't let foreigners in anymore, do they?"

"The organization I work for has connections that allow us to do what we have to. I'm a wizard as are my colleagues. We have resources that we can call on that your average person doesn't. That's also how we found Julian's body."

Mrs. Pilat touched her fingers to her lips. "A wizard, my goodness. I've never met a wizard before. If you hadn't said anything I never would have guessed you were anything more than an ordinary young woman. No offense meant, of course. I just always imagined wizards looking…different, I suppose."

Helena smiled. "I'm not the easily offended sort, madame. Pretty much all wizards are just people who have the fortune, good or bad depending on your point of view, to be able to wield magic."

There was an awkward silence as the two women sipped their tea. At last Helena said, "Is there anything you can tell me about Julian's new job? They are very likely the ones that sent him to Australia. Given the sealed nature of the country, that had to have taken either a very large bribe or powerful magic."

"He didn't say much about them, but if you'd like to look around his room, I left everything the way it was." Her voice caught and she sniffed. "I hoped he might come back eventually."

"I'm sorry to be the bearer of such bad news."

Mrs. Pilat shook her head. "It's not your fault, dear. In my heart I think I just couldn't face what my head knew to be the truth. Now I have no choice but to face it. He's with the archangels now and it won't be long before I join him. Julian's room is upstairs, second on your right. Take all the time you need."

Helena stood, fighting back tears of sympathy. "Thank you very much. And, while I'm sure that it's a small comfort, rest assured that if the people that hired your son turn out to be criminals, they will answer for their crimes."

Mrs. Pilat patted her hand before shuffling out of the dining room with her tea.

Helena swallowed a sigh and went back to the entry room. There was another doorway that led deeper into the house and she felt certain that's where she'd find the stairs.

Sure enough, a set of narrow, steep stairs led to the second floor. She dearly hoped that Mrs. Pilat didn't have to climb them very often. It would be an easy way to break your neck.

At the top she turned right, walked past a bathroom, and stopped in front of an open door. Beyond it was a bedroom. Nothing remarkable was visible and she sensed no magic. The bed was neatly made. A brass lamp sat on a nightstand beside the bed and a chest of drawers rested against the far wall. Helena couldn't have conjured up a more mundane scene if she tried.

Yet somehow the man that called this room home had ended up dead in Australia with a demon seal in his pocket. She had so many questions, the main one being why didn't whoever buried him take the seal, assuming that was the goal of his visit.

Well, that was what she was supposed to figure out. Tearing the room apart would be adding insult to injury, but thankfully a wizard had other means of searching. She closed her eyes and gathered ether around her. With a thought she sent it out in every direction.

The walls were hollow, but there was nothing hidden in the void between rooms. No secret compartments in the dresser or nightstand. Hello, what have we here? There was a paper between the mattress and box spring.

A gesture lifted the mattress up so she could grab it.

When the mattress was back in place she sat and unfolded her prize. It was an ad for a company called Explorers Inc. In the center was an image of a good-looking man dressed in khakis and hiking boots. The text described a job searching for archeological artifacts in exotic locations. Make lots of money and see the world. Sounded like a video game. Exactly the sort of thing a bored young man eager for adventure would be attracted to.

On the bottom was a Paris address and a name, Emile Blaze. Of equal interest was the web address in the top right corner.

Curious, Helena got out her phone. The connection was weak, but she punched in the address anyway. Unfortunately, all she got was a "site not found" error. Not a big surprise but disappointing all the same.

Fortunately, the Circle had their very own hacker extraordinaire. She closed the web browser and dialed the boss.

"Helena." The boss's smoky voice came through loud and clear despite the poor connection. "I hope you have good news. Or at least as good as possible given the nature of your mission."

"I'm not sure how good it is, but I did deliver the news to Mrs. Pilat. She took it about as well as you'd expect. I also found an advertisement for a shady-looking relic recovery business. I figure that's who Julian got mixed up with. I've got a Paris address, but their website is either down or deleted. I was hoping you could ask Crystal to look into it."

"Not a problem, give me the address."

Helena did so. "I'll finish up here then head for Paris. Maybe I can pick up the trail there."

There was a long pause then the boss said, "Alright, but be

careful. If it looks like anything serious, fall back and let me know. I'll send backup."

"Understood. I'll be in touch." She hung up and pocketed both her phone and the ad. It was time to say goodbye to Mrs. Pilat and head for Paris. Helena didn't know what she'd find, but she had a bad feeling about it.

CHAPTER TWO

Before the war, Paris had been known as the City of Lovers. As Helena bounced down rutted streets and did her best not to make eye contact with the many shambling drug addicts lining the streets, she had a hard time picturing it. These days there were sections of the city the police didn't even visit, lawless enclaves where gangs controlled everything. Naturally the address for Explorers Inc. was in one of those enclaves.

Helena had her doubts about the business from the moment she read the flyer she found under Julian's mattress, but once she looked up the address on her phone and got a flashing red warning saying "visit at your own risk," her doubts had only grown. She also hadn't heard back from the boss yet. Though a couple of hours would be quick work even for Crystal.

The thud from a particularly deep pothole rattled her back to full focus. The last thing she needed was a flat.

A quick glance at her phone confirmed that she was getting close. Not that the neighborhood showed any sign of improvement. Well, there were a couple of reasonably sober-looking prostitutes standing on the street corner. That might count as an improvement depending on how generous you were feeling.

She took the next right and her phone beeped. This was the address, but all she saw was a boarded-up storefront in an old brick building that looked like it might collapse at any moment. Explorers Inc. had gone out of business. Or at least relocated. Not a surprise given that their website was deactivated.

Maybe she'd get lucky and find a clue they left behind. Helena smiled to herself as she climbed out of the car. Right, and maybe pigs would sprout wings and become birds.

A simple ward would ensure that her car remained untouched. Just to be on the safe side, she conjured an ethereal barrier around herself as well. With her precautions taken, Helena crossed the street and strode up to the boarded-over building.

First she tried to peer through the gaps in the boards, but it was completely dark inside. If she wanted to learn anything, she was going to have to break in. Maybe ending up in one of the no-go zones would be to her advantage after all. Nobody around here was going to call the police if she smashed the door open.

She yanked the first board off and tossed it aside. The door frame was so rotten that the nails were barely holding. If they had totally abandoned this location, why bother boarding it up in the first place?

Just one more question to add to her collection.

Helena was so focused on her demolition work that she was taken by surprise when something cold touched the back of her neck. A moment later a faint tingle ran through her body.

She spun around and found a pair of grubby men in tattered clothes a couple paces behind her. One carried zip ties and the other a stun gun. The guy with the stun gun was staring at it, a dim look of confusion on his dirty face.

"Kidnapping's illegal," Helena said. "But if you answer some questions, I'll overlook it."

"Breaking and entering is also illegal," Zip Ties said. "The owner of this place pays us to keep people out."

Helena brightened. "Would that be Mr. Emile Blaze? I was hoping to speak with him. I'm investigating the death of one of Explorers Inc.'s employees and I have a number of questions for him."

"He didn't introduce himself, but he did pay us," Zip Ties said. "Too bad for you the stun gun didn't work. Now we're going to have to beat you unconscious. Shame to have to ugly up that pretty face, but the rest of you will still bring a good price at the market."

Helena shook her head. "Do you really think that's how this is going to go?"

She made a circle with her finger and glowing bands of energy bound the two men hand and foot. "I've fought monsters that would make your hair curl and your bladder weak. I assure you, two thugs in a Paris back alley are no threat to me."

Both men were staring at her with fear in their eyes rather than greed. That was good; it meant they had brains enough to know they were outmatched.

Helena pointed at the ground and the magic forced them to sit in the dirt and look up at her. "Here's how this is going to work. I ask questions. You answer them. Lie to me and the bands get tighter. Refuse to answer and the bands get tighter. I'm not sure how long it will take for your arms and ribs to shatter, but I am confident that it will be painful. Do we understand one another?"

Both men gave eager nods.

"Excellent. First question. Where is Emile Blaze?"

"I don't know," Zip Ties said—honestly, more's the pity.

"Then how do you get paid?"

"He comes here every other week, asks us questions, then hands us an envelope full of cash. Always the same questions. Has anyone been sniffing around? Any new people in the neighborhood? Up until you arrived, the answer has been no to both."

So none of Emile's other employees had any loved ones show up looking for answers. Helena refused to believe that Julian had been the only unfortunate to get suckered in by Emile's promises of adventure. Did that mean they didn't have any family who cared enough to look for them or did these two clowns get rid of them the way they tried to get rid of her? Must be the former since they didn't lie about her being the first person to show up.

"When is he due to show up again?"

"He never shows up on the same day. The guy looks terrified of something. Maybe he knows you're looking for him."

Helena hadn't even known that Emile existed yesterday. No, if he was afraid of someone it wasn't her.

"Did he ever go into the building?"

"He never even looked at it," Zip Ties said. "He pulls up in his fancy sedan and gets out, looking every which way like he's ready to bolt at any moment. When we show up, he asks his questions, pays us, and splits as fast as he can."

"How long have you been working for him?"

"About a month. Next time he pays us will be the third time." Zip Ties grimaced. "Not that I expect to get paid again. You'll make sure of that, I imagine."

"You imagine correctly. Thank you for your honesty. I'm going to set you free. Leave your toys behind and go away. If I see you again, it'll be the last time." She snapped her fingers and the bands vanished.

The two thugs dropped the stun gun and ties before fleeing the area as fast as their scrawny legs could carry them. Helena watched them until they were out of sight. Daisuke would shake his head at her for letting them go. They were clearly criminals and would probably get busy victimizing someone new tomorrow. He would've killed them both and disintegrated their bodies. She, however, had always been hesitant to kill. Whether that turned out to be a strength or a weakness long term, time would tell.

Putting the two fools out of her mind, Helena returned to the storefront. She yanked off one more board and finally the opening was big enough to enter.

The first thing she noticed was the reason for the boards. Someone had smashed the door to pieces. A conjured light appeared at her mental command and revealed what had once been a greeting area as well as a meeting space, all of which were in as bad a shape as the door. Maybe her first guess about no one else showing up looking for their loved one was wrong. Whoever did all this was clearly in a rage.

She got busy sifting through the debris, but it soon became apparent that there was nothing to find. A magical search came up equally empty. Annoyed but hardly surprised, Helena stepped back out of the building. She very badly wanted to get out of this neighborhood, but even if she placed a ward to alert her to Emile's arrival, she'd get here too late to catch him.

Pity she couldn't shadow walk like Daisuke and Jinx. That was such a useful trick. Unfortunately, it wasn't only a lack of aptitude for the spell. Helena also lacked the raw power to open a path. Much as she might dislike it, there was no avoiding the truth.

Which left her with one option: a stakeout.

When the last board had been replaced, she looked around the area. The buildings were all in terrible shape, but she sensed people living in them despite that. Maybe the easiest option would be to set up camp on the roof of Emile's building. That would be out of sight and close enough to allow her to act quickly.

She nodded to herself. First she needed to find a parking garage to store her car, then she'd come back on foot with supplies.

A rooftop camp couldn't be worse than sleeping in the outback, right?

CHAPTER THREE

Daisuke had lived in Zurich for a few years and knew the city inside and out. He knew it so well in fact that he no longer got excited walking around the different districts. One of the many things he enjoyed about showing Jinx around was that her enthusiasm at seeing new things made it feel like he was seeing them for the first time as well. The fact that when she laughed and bounced with excitement her ample chest strained the buttons of her blue blouse to near breaking didn't hurt anything either.

They were just finishing up a shopping trip and he was loaded down with bags filled with Jinx's new wardrobe. Before they arrived, all she owned for clothes was a shadow-silk dress that left more skin bare than covered. Daisuke wouldn't have minded if she wore that all the time, but it really drew too much attention.

Jinx turned away from the window display she'd been looking at, her dark hair swirling around her as she spun.

Bright-red lips turned up in a toe-curling smile. "What should we do now?"

"Lunch!" Ruq, his invisible imp familiar, said. "I'm starving to death here."

"You don't even need to eat and it's barely eleven thirty." Daisuke frowned. "Though maybe a bite to eat wouldn't be a terrible idea. What do you think, Jinx?"

The beautiful half demon just shrugged. "I won't need to eat for at least four more days, but whatever you want to do is fine. I'm shopped out. I'm pretty sure I also spent my full advance."

Daisuke grinned. The boss had given Jinx a check for her first two weeks' pay when she agreed to join the Circle of Sorcery as a provisional field agent. Unfortunately, three thousand euros didn't go that far when you had to buy a whole wardrobe. Well, a woman's wardrobe anyway. Every article of clothing Daisuke owned cost less than a grand combined.

"We'll swing by Milliner's Deli and get sandwiches. It's on the way back to the apartment building anyway."

"And cheesecake," Ruq said.

"For sure." No way could they visit Milliner's and not get strawberry cheesecake.

"You two certainly know your food," Jinx said.

"Food is life's second greatest pleasure. I'd be happy to teach you all about the first anytime you'd like." Daisuke grinned and gave a suggestive waggle of his eyebrows.

Jinx's pale skin flushed. Despite being hundreds of years old, a half demon, and a stunning woman, she had surprisingly little experience with sex. In fact, he was pretty sure she had no experience with it. No doubt living in a cave with only your sisters for company did nothing for your social life.

"Do you think Helena's okay?" she asked.

Bringing up the other woman in his life was a perfect way to kill the mood. He didn't know if she did it on purpose or if he just had rotten luck.

"I'm sure she's fine. This isn't a dangerous mission. Physically at least. Emotionally... that's another matter. I'd rather fight a demon than have to tell some parent that their kid is dead. Helena's a talented field agent. If there's trouble, unless it's something major, she can handle it. And if it is something major, she isn't too proud to run away and call for backup."

Daisuke nearly jumped when his phone chose that moment to ring. He didn't believe in omens, but that was pushing it. "Boss?"

"I'm cutting your recovery short. You and Jinx need to get to the shop. I've got a mission for you."

He swallowed a sigh. Only two days' rest. Not nearly enough, but business was business. "Can I at least get lunch and swing by Jinx's apartment to pick up her stuff?"

"Yes. This is important, but not life or death."

Not life or death, that was a nice change of pace. "Great, see you in an hour or so."

"What do you suppose she wants us to do?" Jinx asked.

That was a good question. Daisuke was pretty sure they were supposed to be on alert in case Helena needed backup in France. Either the boss had good news on that front and they weren't needed anymore or whatever came up was important enough that she was willing to take a chance sending them offsite and risk a delayed response to any trouble.

"Heaven knows, but I'm sure it'll be dangerous if she's

sending the two of us." Daisuke frowned. "Then again, I'm pretty sure we're the only agents not on a mission at the moment. Maybe it won't be dangerous and we were just the only option she had."

"A dozen cookies says it's dangerous," Ruq said.

Daisuke wasn't stupid enough to take that bet. But now he wanted cookies as well as cheesecake. Which was no doubt Ruq's plan when he said it.

"Do you need anything besides your shadow-silk dress?" he asked.

"I don't even need that. I'm wearing it under my new outfit."

That was handy, but he still needed to drop off all her stuff at her apartment.

A little less than an hour later, stuffed to bursting and freed of his burdens, Daisuke led the way to the back door of Arcane Books and Trinkets, the business that served as a front for the Circle of Sorcery. He walked up the steps to the back door and waved a hand, deactivating the protective wards. His key opened the deadbolt and he stepped aside to let Jinx go in first. Once she was through he followed, sealing everything up tight behind him.

Taking the lead, he made the short walk to the boss's office. He knocked and a smoky, sexy voice that had no business coming from an angel of any sort, even a fallen one, said, "Come in."

He pushed the door open and found the room surprisingly smoke free. Even more surprising was the person seated in one of the chairs in front of the boss's desk. At barely five feet tall, Crystal, the group's resident computer genius, looked about fifteen despite pushing thirty. Everything about her was tiny, including the round glasses perched on the tip of her nose.

The boss wore a navy-blue suit today which looked lovely with her pale skin and ash-gray hair. Though if he was being honest, much like Helena and Jinx, the boss could make anything look good.

"Crystal, what brings you out of the computer room?" Daisuke asked.

As soon as he spoke to her Crystal started trembling like a Jack Russell terrier in a thunderstorm. Right; good with computers, bad with people.

"Boss?"

The boss sighed. "Helena asked us to do some background research on the people that sent Julian to Australia. There were some technical details that I didn't fully understand, so I asked Crystal to be here in case you or Jinx have any questions."

"I don't even have a cellphone, much less a computer," Jinx said. When everyone looked at her, she blushed. "Sorry. I won't say anything else."

"No. If you have questions be sure to chime in," the boss said. "You're a member of the team now; you have every right to speak up during briefings. That said, please wait until I finish my explanation to ask any questions."

"Yes, ma'am," Jinx said.

"Lay it on us, boss."

"Right. As best Helena could tell, Julian got a job with a company called Explorers Inc. They promised adventure and excitement, exactly what a bored country boy was looking for. She's on a stakeout waiting for the business's owner to show up. The reason she called us was that their website is down."

"Not down." Crystal's voice came out as a barely audible squeak. "It's been erased. Someone tried to delete it from the internet. They must not have realized archives are a thing."

"Deleted, right," the boss said. "Anyway, it looks like the storefront in Paris isn't the only one they operated. Crystal found addresses in three other cities: London, Madrid, and Venice. We don't know if they're old addresses, still active, or what."

"Let me guess," Daisuke said. "You want us to find out."

"Bingo. You've been to all those cities, right? That means you can shadow walk. Shouldn't take more than a day or two that way."

"Yeah, back when I was traveling around Europe, I visited all of them. Been a while though. If the landscape has changed, the places I knew might not be there. Still, I should be able to get close at least. London's the only hard one. The UK might not be closed like Australia, but they do have some pretty rigorous customs rules. If I shadow walk in without the right passport stamp and get caught, it might be an issue."

The boss waved a hand. "Don't worry about it. You won't be operating in the city long enough for there to be a problem. Assuming that your luck isn't absolutely horrendous."

Daisuke raised an eyebrow at that.

"I mean even worse than usual. Just get in there, find out what you can, and get out."

"If you say so. The Metro mages weren't worth a damn last time I visited anyway, so getting away should be simple if it comes to that. What are the addresses?"

Crystal held out a piece of paper that crinkled as her hand shook.

Daisuke took it gently. "Thanks."

He studied the addresses, but nothing stood out as familiar. Well, it was always nice to visit new places. Maybe they'd get lucky and no one would try and kill them today.

CHAPTER FOUR

Daisuke decided to visit Venice first for the simple reason that he wanted to show Jinx the canals and they were generally prettier during the day. Assuming, of course, that there were no bodies floating in them. That was a fairly regular thing in Venice. There was a ton of smuggling in and out of the port and the gangs were always fighting over territory. And that usually ended up being a good thing since no one wanted any particular gang to get control of the entire port.

The trip through the shadow paths took only an instant. His chosen destination, an alley behind a bar he used to hang out at, was devoid of life. Confident that they wouldn't be seen, Daisuke stepped out of a shadow and glanced around. Other than an overflowing dumpster, the alley was empty. The back door to the bar was closed and would stay that way for another few hours, when the waitresses and other staff arrived.

"Why did you say you visited Venice the first time?" Jinx asked when she'd joined him in the alley.

"Business. One of the smaller gangs dealt in magical and supposedly magical artifacts. I wanted to see what they had, not that I could've afforded to buy anything at the time."

"You probably would've just had me steal whatever you wanted." Ruq's disembodied voice came from beside Daisuke's right ear. "Those losers had the worst security."

"Their security was fine as long as they weren't trying to stop a wizard. Half a dozen guys with machine guns are plenty to discourage a regular thief. Anyway, most of their stuff was trash, so we didn't bother hanging around." Daisuke pulled out his phone and opened the map. "Okay, let's see. Explorers Inc. set up shop not far from the docks. Probably made it easy to sneak in whatever goodies their dupes found. Five'll get you ten that they had a deal going with one of the gangs. And I mean something more than just protection."

"I'm afraid I don't know much about this sort of thing," Jinx said. "My family spent little time interacting with human society."

"You'll learn as we go. Your main job is to back me up if there's trouble and provide a distraction should it be necessary."

"Do you think either of those will prove necessary?"

Daisuke shook his head. "No idea. Assuming this outfit really is shutting down, we'll probably find an empty storefront, the same as Helena. Lucky for us, we're not obliged to stake it out and catch whatever rats show up. I hate stakeouts, so boring. Let's go, the docks are only about a quarter mile from here."

They left the stinking alley and stepped out onto the cobblestone street. A few people were lounging around in the shade, mostly old men enjoying their retirement. This wasn't a touristy part of the city. Much as he'd like to really show Jinx around, they didn't have time to play.

They did have to cross one canal. It was about half full and there wasn't a gondola in sight. No bodies either, so that was a plus. They crossed the curved stone bridge and hurried on their way. Daisuke set a pace that he thought of as "person with something to do." Not so quick that he'd attract attention, but fast enough not to waste time. He'd found that when he moved at this pace vendors and prostitutes tended to leave you alone. Not that there were any of either on their chosen route.

"Is it usually this quiet?" Jinx asked.

"This isn't the most popular part of the city." He pointed to where four huge cranes jutted into the sky. "We're close to the industrial area. Nothing cute about this neighborhood. It's all business."

Two streets after the bridge they turned left down a side street. Two small, connected offices, both unlabeled and closed up tight, sat on the corner. The right-hand office was supposed to be Explorers Inc.

"This doesn't seem right," Jinx said.

"Nothing about this has seemed right since we found that dead guy. I'm going to have a look around inside. You keep watch out here with Ruq. This shouldn't take long."

A short-range shadow walk brought him inside the office. He summoned a dim light and found it completely empty. No furniture, no equipment, no nothing. Clearly they weren't going to learn much here. Emile, assuming he ran things at all the storefronts, must have closed this one down before the one in Paris.

Daisuke rubbed his eyes. He'd hoped to avoid having to drop in on his old contacts, but that no longer seemed possible. Explorers Inc. was exactly the sort of business they'd have their eyes on and their claws into.

He slipped back out into the street. "Total dud. Whoever cleaned this place out was thorough. Other than burning the building to the ground, I don't know what else they might have done to obscure the trail."

"So what now, Madrid?" Jinx asked.

"No, I've got some old associates in Venice and I think it might do us good to talk to them. Vito doesn't have a clue when it comes to magic, but he's been on the docks for forty years. If anyone can tell us what happened with Explorers Inc., he can."

"I don't remember this one," Ruq said.

"Before your time. I'd only been out of school for three months when we met. He thought I was a pushover. It didn't take long to convince him otherwise and once I did, we got along fine."

"How much do you think this'll cost?" Ruq asked. "No way does a guy like that talk for free."

"We'll see how reasonable he's willing to be. His answer will help me decide how reasonable I want to be. My expense account can cover a modest bribe, but I also have no qualms about turning his brain inside out should I have to."

Jinx winced. "Harsh."

"Vito's a crook that would sell his mother for a scuffed nickel. The fact that he's less of an asshole than some doesn't make him a good guy. His place is only about six blocks from here. What say we go get reacquainted?"

Vito operated out of a warehouse on the dock, Bombari's Import and Export. It was a legit business, at least on the surface. It was also a front for a smuggling operation that specialized in magic-adjacent artifacts. Magic adjacent was a nice way of saying old junk that looked like it might have something to do with magic. The hope seemed to be that rich collectors would be too stupid to realize they were getting ripped off. On the other hand, plenty of the non-magical pieces looked cool and if you wanted overpriced decor, you could do worse. Considering Vito had been in business for decades, he clearly knew his market.

The docks grew noisier the deeper in you went. The thump of the freighters' big diesel engines, the squeaks and groans of the cranes, and what port would be complete without the cursing of the longshoremen?

"I preferred Warina," Jinx said.

"Me too, but in this job you don't get to pick where you go. If it's any consolation, I've been to way worse places with way worse company."

"It's not, but thank you for saying so. I believe that's the place just ahead."

Yeah, the three-foot-tall letters on the top of the warehouse were pretty hard to miss. The weird thing was that the big double doors were closed tight. Early in the afternoon on a Thursday he should be wide open and eager for business. Something was up.

"Ruq, take a look. I've got a bad feeling."

He felt his familiar moving up and away toward the windows that ran under the warehouse roof.

The warehouse is empty, Master, but there is a nervous-looking, bald fat man holding a gun seated behind a desk at the rear.

Bald, fat, and armed, that had to be Vito, but where was

all his stuff? There had been scores of boxes last time Daisuke visited. One way to find out.

"It looks like Vito ran into some business trouble. Ruq says he's armed and nervous so this might get touchy."

"Regular bullets are hardly a threat to either of us," Jinx said.

"True, but I still don't like getting shot at. I think we'd best shadow walk in and paralyze him. Once he knows it's safe, we can talk."

"I didn't think you could shadow walk to a place you've never been."

"I saw it through Ruq's eyes and at this range it wouldn't really matter anyway. Ready?"

She held out her hand and they stepped through the nearest shadow. An instant later they appeared behind Vito. The stink of sweat and fear mingled with something nastier that Daisuke didn't want to think too closely about. Vito's pudgy frame went rigid when the spell hit him.

Daisuke took the pistol out of Vito's hand and unloaded it. With the danger, such as it was, removed, he released the spell.

"Kill me if you're going to," Vito said. "I won't beg."

"I'm not going to kill you, Tubby."

Vito started swearing in Italian. "I hate that nickname. I ought to kill you just for using it, you squinty-eyed little shit. Who the hell do you think you are anyway?"

"You don't remember me? I'm hurt. I'm probably one of the few actual wizards to ever visit this rat hole you call a business. Daisuke Kugo, ring a bell?"

Vito's eyes narrowed then widened, then scrunched up as his brain struggled to place Daisuke's name. Finally he said,

"No, but I've been under a lot of stress lately. What do you want?"

"Information, specifically about a company called Explorers Inc."

Vito had finally noticed Jinx and wasn't paying Daisuke the least attention. In fact, he was just short of drooling. Not an attractive man to begin with, his current expression wasn't doing him any favors.

Daisuke snapped his fingers right under Vito's great beak of a nose. "Going to need you to focus."

"Who could focus with this vision of loveliness standing in front of him?"

Daisuke let black lightning dance around his fingers. "Would you like me to help you?"

Vito swallowed hard. "No, I find my thoughts steadying already. Explorers Inc. you said? Don't get me started on those pricks. I'm sure they're the source of my current problems."

"I'm listening."

"You know about the new crew that took over the docks?"

Daisuke snorted. "I doubt the Sicilians will let that go for long."

"Who do you think the new guys took out first? They got some kind of weird monster that shrugs off bullets like a duck does rain. That thing took out all their guns and the don's pet wizard didn't last much longer. The only reason I'm still breathing is that I'm too small-time to matter. At least I thought I was."

"What changed?" Daisuke asked. "And what does any of this have to do with Explorers Inc.?"

"I couldn't tell you exactly, I only know that the new crew

showed up a day after the storefront closed and the guy that ran the place split. It was like he knew they were coming. Wish the prick had let me know, not that I would've believed him. Now I'm just waiting for them to come back and finish the job."

"Why not run for it?" Jinx asked.

Vito barked a short, bitter laugh. "Got nowhere to go, sweetheart. This business is it for me. I'm too old and worn out to start over somewhere else and too broke to retire. My hobbies aren't cheap."

Daisuke had no idea what a whore would charge Vito, but however much it was, it couldn't be enough. "I'll bet. Two more questions, then I'll see about your monster problem. Assuming I kill it, are there enough of the old gang around to kick the newcomers out?"

"You kill that thing and I'll call the Sicilians. We'll have the docks back under control in a weekend. And you'll be a made man. No one in the families will ever mess with you. Anything you need, just ask. My word on it."

Daisuke nodded. It never hurt to have people owe you favors. "Okay, my second-to-last question. Did you get the name of the owner of Explorers Inc.? Or failing that can you give me a description?"

"Sure, I got his name. Lyman Blaze. Decent-enough guy if a little twitchy. We did some business together. He treated me fair. Can't ask for more than that."

Some kin of Emile's for sure. Maybe it was a family business.

"What's your last question?" Vito asked.

"Where can I find the monster?"

CHAPTER FIVE

"**A**re you really going to kill a monster for the mob?" Jinx asked when they'd left the warehouse behind. "I thought we were in a hurry."

"We're not in that big of a hurry," Daisuke said. "I'll bet these new arrivals have something to do with Lyman's disappearing act. The timing is too coincidental otherwise. And even if they're completely unrelated, the monster, as Vito calls it, is likely a demon. We can't just leave it running around causing chaos on the docks. It's important not to get so focused on your immediate task that you don't deal with these other issues when they pop up."

"If it is a demon, it might be too strong for the two of us to deal with."

Daisuke smiled at that. "Summoning anything higher than a tier-three demon would require a sacrificial ritual far bigger than anything these people are likely to be capable of. And I've never seen a tier-three demon I couldn't handle."

He turned down a pier. According to Vito, the new arrivals—he didn't seem to know who they were, or if he did he was reluctant to say—had set up in a warehouse on the opposite end of the docks. Hopefully they were well away from where everyone was working. The last thing Daisuke wanted was to get mixed up in a battle with innocent bystanders nearby.

"I've never heard of tiers when it comes to demons before," Jinx said. "How many are there?"

"It's a system the Circle uses. There are ten tiers with the demon lords at tier ten and demon spirits at tier one. Some people say our system isn't divided finely enough, but it's sufficient to give a basic idea of what you're dealing with. At the end of the day, there's so much variation between demons that any system you use is going to be somewhat vague."

Daisuke concentrated on Ruq. He'd sent the imp ahead to scout out the target. That was risky since the demon might sense his presence, but Daisuke considered it worthwhile. There was really nothing worse than walking into a situation blind.

"What tier am I?" Jinx asked.

He considered that for a moment. "It's hard to say. Since you're only a half demon, I'm not sure how our ranking system applies to you. I'd say you're a high tier four, maybe low tier five. Ruq is a high tier one and Vorgon is a middle tier nine if that gives you any sense of where you stand."

I am a solid tier two, thank you very much.

"What are you smiling at?" Jinx asked.

"Ruq. He's disputing my ranking him at tier one even though that's where imps usually end up. Like I said, it's just an estimate."

There's a barrier around the warehouse. The humans are keeping well away from it. There are no ships nearby either.

What sort of barrier?

Fear and forbiddance at a minimum. Nothing lethal that I can sense. It seems targeted at humans, but I'm sure there's a detection element as well. If I get any closer, whoever made the barrier is sure to notice.

That's fine. Keep your distance. We're only a couple hundred yards away.

"This situation just keeps getting more and more interesting." Daisuke explained about the barrier. "It takes a wizard of considerable skill to make a barrier that complex. We might be in for a bigger fight than I thought."

"Maybe the demon created the barrier," Jinx said.

"That would put it solidly in tier four, and the only way to summon a demon that powerful is with a minimum of a hundred sacrifices. You can't do that sort of thing in the civilized world without the authorities getting wise to it. No, I suspect it's either a wizard or an artifact. Either way, we'll know soon enough."

As they approached the target warehouse, it became clear that he needn't have asked Vito for directions. The building looked ordinary enough on the outside, but it fairly seethed with corrupt magic in the ether. What in the world was the Italian government playing at, letting a group like this get their hooks into a major port city? They must have paid off or more likely threatened the mayor into keeping quiet about it.

Kind of pathetic really.

"How do you want to handle this?" Jinx asked.

"I'll knock and see if anyone wants to come out to play. Can you hide in a shadow nearby? When they're focused on attacking me, you can hit them from the flank. These are criminals, so no need to hold back. Though if you get the chance to take a prisoner or two, maybe we can get something useful out of them. Ruq, feel free to take out anyone shooting at me."

He sensed his familiar's excitement at the prospect. It was easy to forget given his somewhat comical nature that Ruq was still a demon and took a demon's pleasure in killing mortals.

I still prefer eating sweets.

I'm well aware. Just make sure you're ready. I have no issue with you killing mortals, as long as you only kill the ones I tell you to.

Jinx vanished, leaving her trousers and blouse behind. Right, he'd forgotten she said she couldn't take regular clothes with her when she became a shadow.

Time to see if anyone was home.

Daisuke shaped what was essentially an ethereal sledgehammer and slammed it into the ward protecting the warehouse. Both constructs exploded into motes of chaotic energy. Looked like the ward was weaker than it first looked. He figured it'd take at least two strikes to bring it down. Not that he was disappointed; weaker enemies were always preferable.

It didn't take long for the warehouse doors to slide open and what was no doubt the monster came roaring out. It was an ugly thing, standing around six feet tall with sinewy arms that hung past its knees and came complete with rending claws. Its face looked like someone had punched it in leaving a fist-sized dent where the mouth and nose should've been. The rest of its body was covered in thick blond fur.

This thing needed to die just so he didn't have to look at it anymore.

The inevitable men with machine guns followed along

behind the demon. None of them even bothered to point their weapons at Daisuke. They must have been confident in their pet despite the fact that he'd already smashed their ward to bits.

The demon focused its caved-in face on Daisuke, the lack of eyes seeming not to trouble it in the least.

It charged.

Right into a chest full of black lightning. The spell blew it backwards ass over elbows where it landed in a heap.

Never one to give an enemy the chance to recover, Daisuke summoned a black disk under the demon and sent more black lightning into it. Five seconds of that and it was reduced to a slowly dissolving puddle of black goo.

Tier three had clearly been overly generous. That thing was two, two and a half tops.

The thugs seemed to get the idea that they were in trouble and opened fire. Bullets pinged off of his personal shield, troubling him no more than the rain might.

One of them went down and Daisuke caught a glimpse of Ruq before he disappeared again.

Black webs appeared out of nowhere and caught a pair of gunmen, dropping them to the ground.

The rest decided that they'd had enough and turned to run. Daisuke slashed his finger through the air and sent shadow blades flying out to cut them down. In a couple of minutes he was the only one visible still on his feet.

Jinx appeared from a nearby shadow and Ruq landed on his shoulder.

"Pathetic," Ruq said. "I had higher expectations."

"They did seem rather weak," Jinx agreed as she put her blouse back on.

Daisuke swallowed a sigh. While weak as demons went,

that thing would make short work of any normal person that ran into it. Had he been capable of feeling pity for a demon, he might have felt bad for this one. After having such an easy time with the mafia guys, it probably thought it was invincible. Either that, or whoever punched its face in damaged what passed for its brain.

"Let's have a chat with the prisoners and see if they know anything useful. Since no one flung a spell at us, I assume the wizard that summoned that demon and raised the barrier is absent."

Daisuke led the way to the warehouse, pausing long enough to conjure a disk under the two thugs bound in Jinx's shadow webs. They were so totally wrapped up in the black threads that they couldn't even wiggle around.

Inside, the warehouse was filled with crates. Daisuke also sensed a single life force, a weak, unmoving one behind a pile of boxes stacked four high. He angled that way and sure enough found an unconscious man in a very nice charcoal-gray suit lying on the cement. He certainly looked the part of a criminal, but not an Italian one. Daisuke guessed this guy was from further north, assuming his pale skin and dirty-blond hair were any indication.

"Master, his ring," Ruq said.

Daisuke hadn't even gotten to his magical search, but when he did, the black ring on the man's right middle finger gave off a lingering aura of corruption. Was he a wizard after all? Seemed unlikely.

"Won't the authorities come to investigate all this racket?" Jinx asked.

"Not if they've been paid off. They'll keep their distance until their real employer sends word that some bodies need to be cleaned up. That's my theory at least." Daisuke helped himself to the black ring. "Maybe set a shadow to keep watch just in case."

Jinx beamed, seeming pleased to have a task. "Will do."

Gray Suit was likely in charge, might as well start with him.

Daisuke patted his cheek a couple times. "Come on, Sunshine, wake up."

No response.

A sharp crack rang out when he backhanded the unconscious criminal. That drew a groan and slowly the man's eyes opened. They nearly bugged out of his head when he saw Daisuke looming over him.

"What? Who?"

Daisuke shook his head. "No, no, that's not how this works. You lost the fight, which means *I* ask the questions and *you* answer them. Understand? Let's start with your name."

"Do you know who I am? You're dead, both of you."

Daisuke smacked him again. "Your demon's been sent back to whatever hell spawned it. Your thugs are either dead or captured. Only two possibilities remain. One, you answer my questions like a good boy and I stop your heart when we're through. Or, I turn you over to the Sicilians."

Gray Suit's already pale skin had turned bone white. "You can't turn me over to them. You don't know what they'll do to me. Anything would be better than that."

"I actually have a pretty good idea what they'd do and I further suspect you'd deserve all of it and then some. So what's it going to be?"

"My name is Salvo Veiss."

"Much better. I assume you're not a wizard, which makes me wonder where you got your hands on a demon."

"I bought it from the Devil Man. Damn monster cost me a hundred slaves, but it was worth it. With that thing in the lead, we took over the docks in a week. No one could touch us, not until you showed up anyways."

Daisuke had never heard of the Devil Man and didn't like the sound of it a bit. Someone selling bound demons to criminals was bigger trouble than he liked to think about. It seemed he was going to have a lot of stuff to report after they finished up.

"What's your interest in Explorers Inc.?"

"Personally, I couldn't give a shit about them, but the Devil Man said if we could bring him the head of any of the Blaze boys, he'd upgrade our demon at no cost. Don't know what those fools did to piss him off, but the Devil Man wants those brothers in a bad way."

"How many are there?"

"Four, one for each of their locations. That was another reason I chose to make my move on Venice. Seemed like a twofer, you know? But the son of a bitch was gone when we went to his place."

Daisuke shook his head. "That is what you get for being greedy and evil. Where can I find the Devil Man?"

Salvo stared at him. "You want to go up against the Devil Man? You're nuts, kid. I approached him as a paying customer and even then it was all I could do to put one foot in front of the other."

"Your concern for my wellbeing is noted, now answer the question."

"Your funeral. He and his crew operate out of an old castle in Romania. I only saw ten people, at least I assume they were people, when we visited. They all wore these long, hooded robes that hid their features. Creepy bunch, let me tell you."

Daisuke had a sick feeling. "Not Castle Ravenclaw."

"Yeah, you heard of it?"

"Unfortunately. Your cooperation has been most appreciated." Daisuke pointed at his chest.

"Wait!" Salvo said. "You're really just going to kill me?"

"That was my plan. Unless you'd prefer to have the Sicilians do it. I'm fine with that too."

"Couldn't you just let me go? I cooperated and everything."

"No, I can't just let you go. You're a criminal, certainly a murderer, and worst of all, you're apt to warn the Devil Man that I'm interested in him. Now go join your men in hell." Daisuke wrapped a tentacle of ether around Salvo's heart and squeezed.

The man shuddered and went limp, his life force quickly fading away. Daisuke straightened and pocketed the black ring. "I think we're about done here. I'll tell Vito the demon's gone and we can head back to Zurich."

"What about Madrid?" Jinx asked.

"We'll get there, though I hold out little hope of running into one of the Blaze brothers. First I want to drop off Salvo's ring. Our expert can analyze it and give me an idea about what sort of magic the Devil Man uses."

"Want me to finish off the prisoners?" Ruq asked.

"Nah, we'll leave them for Vito and his guys. They might as well do some work. Let's get out of here, I find myself in serious need of pastries."

Daisuke had hoped to never have to return to Castle Ravenclaw, but it looked like his hopes were going to be dashed.

CHAPTER SIX

After a quick stop at Stein's Bakery to load up on sugar, Daisuke and his companions headed straight for headquarters. It was late afternoon in Zurich and the streets were crowded with people shopping, coming home from work, and generally living their lives like demons and hellpriests weren't a thing. Sometimes he thought ignorance really was bliss.

Swallowing a sigh, he turned a corner and headed down the street that led to Arcane Books and Trinkets. The boss wasn't going to be thrilled with his news or the fact that he'd left the mission only a third finished to report back in person, but Daisuke didn't care. He really wanted to know more about the ring he'd taken from Salvo. And while he could analyze it himself, it would take hours of quiet study. Not exactly the best use of his time.

"What's so bad about this castle?" Jinx asked. "I never seen you look so grim, including when you were controlling Vorgon."

Daisuke gave a full-body shudder and did his best to

dispel the gloom he felt. "A lot of bad memories and one good one. That castle is where I found Ruq locked in a cage and left to die."

"Would locking a demon in a cage actually kill it? I mean, he doesn't need food or water right?"

"It'll kill you if the resident high priest of Abaddon puts a siphon spell on it," Ruq said. "That spell was slowly draining my essence in the most painful way possible. If Daisuke hadn't formed a contract with me, I would've been destroyed despite being free."

"The worst part is, the son of a bitch got away," Daisuke said. "Actually, got away isn't the right way to describe it. The high priest was gone when I showed up. The dregs he left behind didn't last long once I decided they needed killing. My fear is that this Devil Man is actually that same priest of Abaddon."

"And that's especially bad, why?" Jinx asked.

"Hellpriests draw power directly from their patron demon lord," Ruq said. "They don't have the same limits as a wizard. They have different limits, but trying to figure them out before you get burned to a crisp by hellfire is no easy task. Assuming this is the same person, I've got a pretty good idea how strong he is. Not unbeatable, but tough enough that you wouldn't want to fight him if you could avoid it."

"Plus heaven knows how many demons he's summoned and cultists he's gathered to his cause," Daisuke added. "One on one I'm not afraid of anybody, but even I can't beat a small army of demons and magic users."

"It wouldn't be one on one," Jinx said.

Daisuke grinned and gave her hand a squeeze. "Thanks."

They reached the back of the shop and Daisuke let them in. He was going to have to get Jinx a key at some point, but it wasn't a huge priority. Once inside they made the short walk to the boss's office and he knocked.

"Come in."

Daisuke pushed the door open and found the boss with her nose stuck in the Book of Wisdom. She read it on a regular basis, so that wasn't strange in and of itself, he just hoped it didn't mean another prison had popped up.

"There's no way you finished your mission already," she said. "What happened?"

Daisuke gave her the condensed version and set the black ring on her desk. "I don't know for sure it's the same priest that escaped, but if Donny can analyze the ring and confirm that it is Abaddon's magic, that would pretty much cinch it."

The boss reached out to touch the ring then stopped. "I can feel the leftover corruption. It's a wonder the human that wore it didn't lose a finger. I'll get Donny started right away. In the meantime, don't do anything rash. You've still got to check Madrid and London and you're Helena's backup if anything happens."

"No need to tell me, boss," Daisuke said. "I'm happy to put off a return trip as long as possible. Still, I have no doubt we'll need to deal with this so-called Devil Man sooner or later. Organized crime and tame demons are a bad combination."

The boss snorted. "That's an understatement. Be careful, Daisuke. Something about this is giving me the willies."

"Is that a roundabout way of saying you got a divine revelation?"

She pointed at the door. "Get back to work."

Daisuke grinned. Come what may, he felt better having made his report. Now it was time to see what sort of trouble they could get into in Madrid.

Remi Velung, better known to the Cult of Abaddon as the Devil's Shadow, rubbed the bridge of his nose. One of the demons they sold to raise operating capital had been destroyed. He didn't know the details, but he did feel the backlash from its banishment, thus the faint headache currently plaguing him. He reached for the half-full tumbler on his desk and downed the Scotch. That didn't help the headache at all, but he did enjoy the burn.

His office in Castle Ravenclaw was nothing to get excited about, but it had everything he needed for his work. And it was brilliant work. Not even Solomon the Great had thought to fuse the demons with a mask to allow a human to bond with and control them. That was all Remi. There were risks of course, particularly to the wearer's sanity, but these cultists were already insane, so that wasn't an issue.

He sighed and pushed away from his desk. Probably best to tell the high-and-mighty Devil Man about the demon's destruction. Delaying would only make his mood worse. The high priest of Abaddon, Remi still didn't know the man's real name. He wasn't sure anyone here did. Not that it mattered, Devil Man suited the fanatic perfectly.

Luckily for his throbbing head, the walk to the Devil Man's room was a short one. All but one of their agents was in the field at the moment, so there was little for the leaders of the cult to do. Not that Remi considered himself a true member. These fools were just expendable tools to further his research. When the time came, he would happily slaughter the lot of them.

The door to the Devil Man's room had a bronze knocker in the shape of a demon skull surrounded by flames. Ugly thing, but it served its purpose well enough. Remi knocked a few times and soon the door opened.

The Devil Man had discarded his black robe and wore only shorts. His bare chest was covered with singed black hair and numerous burn scars. His face, at least, had been spared such treatment. His square jaw appeared freshly shaved and his hard gray eyes were narrowed as he looked down on Remi.

"What is it?" his deep, sonorous voice boomed out. It was the perfect tone for someone that spent most of their time trying to inspire the troops. Had he not been a demon-worshipping lunatic, the Devil Man would've made a fine politician. If he was being honest, the demon-worshipping-lunatic thing wasn't even disqualifying for most political positions.

Right. Focus, Remi. "One of the demons we sold was just killed. Figured you'd want to know."

The Devil Man's thick brows drew down. "Does this affect the rest of our plan?"

"I don't see how it could. We sold them the demon, not a guarantee of invincibility. Besides, what are they going to do, complain?"

A slow smile spread across the Devil Man's face. "Fair point. Have you heard anything from the rest of the team?"

"My bound servant hasn't reported anything new. As for Nicholas and Velcan, neither of them talks to me if they can avoid it. I'm not sure why. Do I strike you as especially frightening?"

The Devil Man laughed at that. "No. They prefer to report to me because they want praise for their efforts. And since I haven't heard from them, I assume that means they've accomplished nothing of note."

Remi nodded. That sounded about right. "I'll let you get back to whatever you were doing."

"I was contemplating the glory of Abaddon. You never did tell me why you decided to join my cause. You have no faith, that much is painfully obvious."

"I thought I explained myself clearly. Your goals and my research intersect perfectly. You provide me with subjects and I provide you more power. When the greater demon is freed, I expect that you'll live up to our agreement and provide me with whatever research subjects and resources I require."

"If you can grant me Razak's power, have no doubt that you shall be rewarded exactly as you wish." The Devil Man rubbed his hands together. "We will all get exactly what we wish for."

Remi bowed. "Splendid. I shall return to my lab and await good news."

He turned on his heel and marched back the way he'd come. He didn't trust the Devil Man any more than he did his former master. When the time came, Remi would seize his fate with his own hands.

CHAPTER SEVEN

After their meeting with the boss, Daisuke and Jinx had set out for Madrid. For better or worse, that turned out to be a dud. They found the Explorers Inc. storefront, but it was already in the process of being renovated for a new tenant. Jinx had done a fine job of convincing one of the contractors on duty to dish what little he knew about the former tenant. Long story short, Timothy Blaze mailed the keys to the building back to the owner without so much as a fare-thee-well and vanished to parts unknown.

Probably a good idea if the Devil Man was after his head.

Jinx gave the besotted construction worker a friendly wave and joined Daisuke at a bench across the street. "You heard everything?"

"Yeah, disappointing, but not exactly a shock. Maybe we'll have better luck with Blaze number four, but I'm not holding my breath. Clearly the brothers know they're being hunted and are lying low. Smart, but I can't figure out what Emile is thinking, poking his head out once a week to check on that storefront. Hopefully Helena can get us some answers."

"So are we good to go to London?"

"Not yet. I want to get there after dark. At night, the police will be too busy with real crime to bother with a couple of out-of-towners not causing trouble. During the day, some patrolman with an overdeveloped sense of responsibility might ask to see our passports. And since mine won't have the right stamp and as far as I know you don't even have one, that would be a problem."

"I suppose," Jinx said. "It just feels wrong sitting here when we have a task in front of us."

"I swear sometimes waiting is half the job. If you think we've got it bad, just imagine poor Helena having to keep watch on an empty storefront for heaven only knows how long. We only need to wait a couple more hours."

"As long as we're waiting, we should eat," Ruq said.

That wasn't a terrible idea. If there was trouble, the extra energy would do Daisuke good. They ended up wandering around downtown Madrid for three hours before the sun had fully set. Belly full and ready for action, Daisuke took Jinx's hand and strode through the nearest shadow.

They emerged a moment later in a busy London entertainment district. The noise from a number of clubs blared out into the street along with flashing lights. Hundreds of young people were out and about, dressed in their finest and, in the women's cases, skimpiest clothes. The street was lined with bars and restaurants, all of which seemed to be doing a brisk business. Not bad considering it was still relatively early.

"I've never been anywhere like this." Jinx's eyes were wide and staring, trying to take in everything at once.

"Yeah, London's something. Lots of money in this town, some of it even legal. Much as I'd like to take you dancing, we need to focus." Daisuke pulled his phone out and brought up a map. He plugged in the Explorer Inc. address. It was in a completely different neighborhood, a good three miles from here. "Looks like we're going for a walk."

Jinx shrugged. "It's a nice night for it."

When he tried to let go of her hand Jinx held on tight. Daisuke smiled and they set out. When they'd put most of the noise behind them and entered a quieter business district Jinx asked, "Why did you pick such a busy area for our arrival point?"

"Because everyone there was either drunk, high, or looking for a hookup. I probably could've cast a fireball into the air and they'd have thought it was fireworks. Sometimes the best way to avoid notice is to be the least interesting thing in a very busy place."

Daisuke set a brisk but steady pace. His gaze darted all around, looking for anything that might be a threat. Not that he and Jinx had anything to fear from muggers, but he still preferred not to take anything for granted. There *were* criminal wizards after all.

"What—" Jinx's question was cut off when a scream tore through the night. Shrill and high pitched, it had to be a woman.

Daisuke only hesitated for a moment. The likely empty business wasn't going anywhere, and he couldn't just ignore someone in trouble.

He lunged forward, sprinting toward the scream.

Another one rang out. Closer now. Down an alley just ahead.

He rounded the corner and found two men trying to

wrestle a struggling woman wearing a cocktail dress into the back of a white panel van. Talk about a clichéd getaway vehicle.

A paralysis spell hit all three of them, sending the group crashing to the ground.

"Why'd you zap the girl?" Jinx asked.

"No choice. They were so close together and in physical contact that the spell recognized them as one target. I doubt she'll complain too loudly given the alternative. Ruq, stay here and keep an eye out. I don't want to be interrupted."

He sensed Ruq fly onto a nearby roof, still invisible. From there he'd be able to see anything coming well before it arrived. That done, he led the way over to the rigid pile of people. The spell allowed nothing beyond the automatic functions that maintained your life.

Daisuke summoned a dim golden light then got to work carefully freeing the girl from his spell while keeping the other two bound. When he finished, she went limp then quickly scrambled to her feet. She looked from her would-be kidnappers to Daisuke and Jinx as if uncertain if her situation had improved.

"Please stay calm," Daisuke said. "I'm not going to hurt you. My name's Daisuke. Are you hurt?"

"I...No, I'm okay. Those guys grabbed me on the way to the club. I know I shouldn't be walking alone, but I had to visit the loo and my friends went ahead. I'm a student at the London School for Wizards. I guess they figured I'd be okay."

"You're a wizard?" Daisuke couldn't see so much as a spark of magic around her.

"A student, first year. I just barely learned how to see the ether and the swirly lights make me sick to my stomach so I can't look for long. I can't even make a light, much less defend myself." She sounded bitter and Daisuke didn't blame her. The start of one's journey into magic was always the most frustrating part.

"I'm sure you'll get there if you keep at it."

"That's what my teachers say. Suppose I should give the bobbies a shout."

"Could you give me fifteen minutes alone with these assholes? Also, if you could avoid mentioning that I saved you, that would be great."

Her brown eyes narrowed. "Are you in some kind of trouble?"

"No, but I don't like dealing with the police. I figured since I saved your life, you could help me out in return."

Her expression softened. "I suppose you did at that. Sure, fifteen minutes and I never got a look at whoever helped me. As soon as I got loose, I ran for it. Sound good?"

"Sounds perfect, but keep your testimony to a minimum if you can. Even a Metro mage can spot lies."

She giggled then slapped a hand over her mouth. "I shouldn't laugh. They catch so much crap doing an awful job, but they really aren't very talented, are they?"

"Not unless they've improved a great deal since my last visit to the city. Good evening, miss."

"Good evening and thank you for saving me." She smoothed her skirt and hurried down the alley out of sight.

Daisuke shook his head. He couldn't decide if she was brave or stupid to be walking through this part of town alone at night. Dismissing the thought as irrelevant, he turned to Jinx. "I'll question them while you check the back of the van."

"What am I looking for?"

"Anything interesting. I'm sure you'll know it when you see it."

Jinx looked dubious but headed for the van while Daisuke went over to the still-paralyzed would-be kidnappers and crouched. A sound barrier fell in place around them and a minor adjustment to the spell freed their heads.

"Okay, fellas, I don't have much sympathy for kidnappers on the best of occasions, so what say you tell me what the big idea was? And please don't lie. I generally dislike inflicting pain on people, but in your cases I'll make an exception."

Both men just glared at him, their expressions cold and unimpressed. They had the hard faces of men that had seen and done plenty of ugly things. It seemed a bit of coaxing was going to be required.

"Have it your way, but don't say I didn't warn you." Daisuke formed a blade of compressed ether and colored it black so the pair could see it as it floated closer to the right-hand kidnapper's face. "You look like you could use a shave. I don't have the best control with this spell so I might get a little skin as well. Feel free to scream. No one can hear you."

Daisuke set the edge of his enchanted blade against the skin of the man's cheek then pressed just a bit harder. He'd lied about having poor control. He could peel a grape without nicking the flesh if he wished to.

The magical blade dug in just a hair then started slicing the skin off, stubble and all. The kidnapper grimaced, which only made the blade dig in deeper. A low moan slipped out as Daisuke sliced the first inch of skin off. When he had most of a second inch peeled the kidnapper screamed.

"Stop! I'll tell you everything. Please, just stop cutting."

"Shut your fuckin gob, Jenkins. You know what the boss—"

Daisuke replaced the paralysis spell on kidnapper number two's head, cutting him off mid-threat. "Thank you. I'm all ears. And if I don't like what you have to say, I'll cut yours off." He added that last bit in the most lighthearted, cheerful tone he could manage. As if cutting someone's ears off was something he did on a regular basis and thus no big deal. That tone often worked better than a more threatening one.

"Sure, look, it's not that complicated, right? Someone's offering big money for wizards, but they gotta be alive. Don't ask me who, I'm just muscle. No one tells me anything I don't need to know. The boss gave us a list of students from the magic school. Figured the ones just getting started would be easier to snatch. See how that worked out."

"Are you the only group looking for students?"

"No, there are two other teams. I don't know where they went to hunt. We all got our lists and went our separate ways, right? No one wanted to share their bonus."

The casual way he said bonus, as if kidnapping and selling innocent kids into heaven knew what sort of hell was just like a sales job, brought Daisuke to the boiling point. But he kept a tight rein on his anger. He needed more information. Much as he'd like to kill these pieces of shit, he had to hold off for a few more minutes.

"Tell me where I can find your boss."

"Sure. We own a warehouse in the Sty." He rattled off an address. "Our gang works out of there. Look, I didn't want to do this, you know? But our boss isn't the sort of person you refuse, right? He'd kill me as soon as look at me and I'd be replaced in an afternoon. No shortage of desperate people in the Sty."

Daisuke nodded. He'd visited the Sty on business once and had hoped never to do so again. It was the worst part of London by a lot. The police didn't even try to enforce law and order. They'd be slaughtered if they did.

"Thank you very much for your help." Daisuke ran a thread through Kidnapper One and into Kidnapper Two before sending a massive bolt of black lightning along it, burning the life out of both of them. It was a cleaner death than they deserved, but Daisuke really wasn't the sadistic sort.

"I found the list he mentioned," Jinx said as she emerged from the back of the van. "We're racking up quite a body count this mission."

Daisuke shrugged and accepted the list. "More dead criminals is generally a good thing. This pair was worse than most since they target the weak. I hate bullies."

He increased the power to his light before snapping a picture of the list. They had pictures and everything. Fifteen young men and women whose only crime was being born a wizard were on there. Hopefully the boss could get word to the school so they could at least alert the targets.

His picture went off along with a brief explanatory text and a promise to call after they visited Explorers Inc.

"We're going there first?" Jinx had been reading over his shoulder.

"It's on the way and I doubt it'll take more than fifteen minutes to look the place over. Given what we've found so far, I'm less than optimistic that we'll find anything useful."

"I'd like to make an argument for our success, but I'm

forced to agree. The Blaze brothers did a good job hiding their tracks."

"Nothing like having someone calling himself the Devil Man on your trail to focus the mind. I just hope we find them before the other hunters. Something tells me whatever those brothers got into, it's bad. Hopefully not end-of-the-world bad, but in this line of work, it pays to assume the worst. Let's go."

CHAPTER EIGHT

Angelique looked around her somewhat austere office and sighed. She had a perfectly nice apartment in one of the more exclusive buildings in Zurich. Why she bothered with it was another question since she seldom left the office. As a fallen angel, it wasn't like she actually needed to sleep or eat. In the end, she supposed it came down to wanting to feel more human. As if owning an apartment she never visited would do that.

She stretched, snatched the pack of cigarettes off her desk, and pulled one out. She felt nothing when she pulled the smoke deep into her lungs. It was all habit and show, just like much of what she did.

Before she could flick the lighter her phone beeped, signaling the arrival of a text from Daisuke. He had his own tone since whatever he was working on was usually the most dangerous mission at the moment. Tossing her cigarette away, she grabbed the phone and swiped it open. There was a picture of a list of names and a short note.

How had he gotten mixed up in a kidnapping? She swore

that boy had the worst luck. Or maybe it was good luck, since he usually ended up saving someone, like that student tonight. Angelique liked to think of it as the luck of Solomon. But if it was, then their enemies had it as well. A couple of taps sent the image to her printer, which whirred to life.

Though far from necessary, Angelique preferred hard-copies. Something about the feel of the paper helped her concentrate. She took the warm paper off the printer and started reading. Not that there was much detail, just names and pictures. Daisuke always assumed that she knew everyone and she kept telling him she didn't, but in this case, luck was on their side. Angelique had an acquaintance in the Metro police. She could get the details to the right person and more importantly she wouldn't ask any uncomfortable questions about how Angelique came by the information.

A couple of clicks and swipes sent the info on its way. With any luck the police could find and secure the students before anyone got seriously hurt. There weren't that many names on the list, so it shouldn't be too big of a job.

That done, she pushed away from her desk and stood. She hadn't heard from Donny or Crystal in a while, time to check in and see how they were doing. A short walk down the hall brought her to the stairs to the basement. At the bottom she stopped before two doors. The left-hand door led to Crystal's computer lab. It had the latest and greatest technology, much of it built by Crystal herself.

Though far from stupid, Angelique only understood about a third of what Crystal said when she described her equipment and what it could do. The words sounded more like magic than some of the actual magic they dealt with on a regular basis.

The right-hand door led to Donny's lab, a far different set up than the tech-heavy computer room. She seldom visited as Donny had an extreme fear of other people, even people he knew meant him no harm. In truth, he left his lab even less often than Crystal, going so far as to sleep and eat there so he didn't have to face other people. Donny made Crystal seem downright outgoing in comparison.

Best to get the hard one out of the way first. She knocked on Donny's door. "Status report, please."

She crossed her arms and waited. It always took a few minutes. Today wasn't as bad as sometimes. About five minutes after she spoke, a slip of paper slid out from under the door. She picked it up and read. *"Preliminary results suggest wizardry not demonic magic. Still too soon to say for sure."*

Interesting. If the preliminary results held, that meant the Devil Man wasn't the missing hellpriest of Abaddon. Whether that was better or worse, she wasn't yet certain. A wizard powerful enough to create artifacts and bind demons to them was certainly not someone to be underestimated. Of course, once he completed his tests, Donny might well come to a different final conclusion. That was the problem with preliminary results, they could always change.

Angelique pocketed the piece of paper and moved to the other door. She knocked and let herself in. If Crystal was really into something, she was apt to not even notice when someone rapped on the door. Since, unlike Donny, Crystal was merely introverted and not genuinely terrified of people, there was no problem with just walking in.

The first thing she always noticed in the computer room was the hum. There were racks upon racks of technical gizmos. Angelique had no idea what most of them did, but she did find the noise they emitted annoying.

She found Crystal seated in front of the main computer console, staring at a monitor easily three feet across and covered with dozens of open browser windows. While she might not be a wizard, Crystal's ability to focus on multiple tasks at once with no loss of cognitive ability was a unique ability in its own right. Angelique wouldn't have been shocked to discover she had a wild talent, not that Crystal would ever be willing to sit for a proper analysis.

"Status report, please," Angelique said.

Crystal nearly jumped out of her chair before turning to look at Angelique through thick glasses that magnified her bloodshot eyes. "You startled me."

"I knocked before I came in. Find anything?"

"Not about Explorers Inc. Not much about the Blaze brothers either for that matter. If they had social media accounts, they've been deleted and scrubbed by someone that knew their business. I do have a bit of historical information. They were born in Scotland. Their ages range from thirty-two to forty. No other living family, at least that I can find. No indication that any of the brothers has magical aptitude. As for the company, it was incorporated in London five years ago, stated purpose being exotic tourism."

Angelique snorted. "That's an interesting way to describe relic hunting. Or maybe that part of the business came later."

"Couldn't say, they never updated their corporate records online. Not that they have to." Crystal sounded annoyed at that. Probably because if it wasn't online, she couldn't find any information. "I'm happy to keep digging if you want, but I'm pretty sure I've found all there is to find from this end."

"If you're confident, then so am I. What about Castle Ravenclaw?"

"Yeah, that place is a problem." Crystal typed in a command and the screen went blank.

"What happened?"

"This is what the satellite sends back when I point it at the castle. There's some kind of barrier concealing everything within a mile of the place. Tech can't get through it. Might as well be a black hole."

"Pull back. Let's see the landscape around the castle."

Crystal tapped a key three times and the darkness grew smaller as fields and trees appeared around it. No sign of civilization. Not that she blamed them. Who in their right mind would want to live within five miles of a demon-haunted ruin. Romania didn't have much in the way of a central government either. The country was basically wild land, where people could come and go as they pleased and do what they wanted.

"Can you put some kind of a program together that would send an alert whenever someone came or went from that black area?"

"Sure, that's a five-minute job. Anything you want me to do when I finish?"

"Get some rest. If Daisuke gets some new intel, we'll need you clearheaded and ready." Crystal gave a little shiver when Angelique said Daisuke's name. "Does he frighten you? Daisuke would never harm an ally."

"He doesn't exactly frighten me so much as make me nervous." Angelique raised an eyebrow at that. "Okay, more nervous than most people make me. He has an aura, a darkness about him. I can't explain it better than that."

Angelique had never felt anything of the sort from Daisuke, but she wasn't about to question Crystal's reaction. Everyone was different after all.

"Well, try to get some sleep. I'm afraid that when things get hot, they're going to get really hot."

Crystal offered a wan smile at that. "What else is new? I'll be ready."

Angelique didn't doubt that in the least. Her team was the best, and they needed to be, given the likely outcome of failure on a mission. Sometimes, death was far from the worst thing you could face.

CHAPTER NINE

Just as Daisuke feared, the London location of Explorers Inc. ended up being a bust. The place was locked down tight and the inside had been cleaned out. There wasn't so much as a crumpled-up piece of paper left in the waste bin.

They emerged from the shadow cast by a lonely street-light. This part of the city was dead quiet at this time of night, which suited him perfectly well. The fewer people they had to deal with the better.

Daisuke glared at the old-style brick building as if it was to blame for his failure to find anything useful. Other than saving that unfortunate young lady, London was turning into as big a bust as Madrid.

"Well, you were right," Jinx said when they'd finished their search. "It's like they scrubbed the place down when they left."

"This is one time I would've been just as happy to be wrong. Looks like it's down to Helena to find the Blaze brothers." Daisuke pulled out his phone. "Assuming nothing's happened in the last half hour, it's time for us to go hunting kidnappers."

Daisuke dialed and after a moment the boss said, "Anything interesting?"

"Not at Explorers Inc. The place was spotless. Unless there's something you need us to do, Jinx and I are going hunting."

"No, all's quiet in Paris. Last time Helena checked in she sounded bored. Not the worst thing in the world. Hopefully Emile shows up soon and we can finally get some answers."

"Answers would certainly be nice. I'll check in when we're finished."

"Daisuke, wait. I also got Donny's preliminary analysis on the ring. He says it looks like wizardry not demon magic."

"Huh, so the Devil Man isn't the hellpriest of Abaddon. A rare bit of good news. At least I think it's good news. Time will tell. Anything else, boss?"

"No. Be careful."

"You know me."

"I do. That's why I'm warning you to be careful."

Daisuke laughed. "Will do, boss. So long."

He hung up and pocketed his phone.

"Something stinks," Ruq said. "There's no way some random wizard just showed up at Castle Ravenclaw and decided to start summoning and binding demons. I suspect that human screwed up."

"She did say the results were preliminary, but when it comes to analyzing magical items, Donny is the best in the business. He might find more information as he works, but there's no way he screwed up. Whatever the case, dealing with it is still a fair ways down the road. Right now, we've got kidnappers on our to-do list. It's time for a visit to the Sty."

"How bad is it going to be?" Jinx asked.

"The fight or the smell?" Daisuke said.

"There's a smell?" Jinx grimaced, her nose crinkling in the most adorable way.

"Oh yeah. A hearty mélange of rotten fish and human waste."

Daisuke set out. The edge of the Sty was about twenty blocks away and the address the helpful kidnapper had provided was near the center. Prime real estate for a criminal operation. Whoever was in charge had to have some serious pull with the local gangs.

They left the businesses behind and passed through a residential area. There were shouts from a bunch of kids playing soccer under the lights nearby, but otherwise the area was quiet. He appreciated that as soon enough it was going to get noisy.

"We might need some backup for this one, assuming we don't want to leave a trail of corpses as we go," Daisuke said. "Can you summon some shadows and have them deal with any thugs that try to slow us down? We only want them unconscious unless they're an actual threat."

Jinx frowned. "I thought you said dead criminals were a good thing."

"Generally, yes. And if they're actively trying to kill you, feel free to kill them back. But if someone's just getting in the way or making a nuisance of themselves, unconscious is fine. It might end up being one of those life lessons that turns them around."

"Really?"

"Probably not, but at a bare minimum it might keep them from attacking a less patient wizard and that can only be a good thing for everyone."

She laughed then frowned. "Is joking before a fight the best idea?"

"Why wouldn't it be?" Daisuke caught a whiff of the Sty drifting on the evening breeze. Not far now.

"It just seems like we should be getting focused, psyching ourselves up or something."

"She's been watching MMA interviews," Ruq said. "It's cutting into my infomercial time. Why is she even watching TV in our apartment at night? She has her own apartment."

"I get lonely. It didn't use to bother me, but now that I've had company, I find I hate being by myself. The noise doesn't keep you awake, does it?"

"No. I just put up a sound barrier. Ruq watches TV all night anyway, so I'm used to it. If spending the nights in my living room makes you feel better, by all means stay whenever you want. Though it could be awkward if Helena sleeps over. We're here."

Daisuke paused and looked over the buildings on either side of them. They'd been deteriorating steadily as they walked, but now looked like they were leaning against each other and that was all that kept them from falling over. The stench had gotten worse.

"Even Abaddon's hell didn't smell this bad," Ruq said. "How can humans live like this?"

"We're remarkably adaptable. We can live just about anywhere. We can't necessarily thrive everywhere, but that's another subject. Can you sense them?"

"About a dozen adolescents watching from the shadows of that tenement to our left?" Ruq said. "Yeah, I sense them. Looks like they're trying to work up the guts to mug us."

"Sounds about right. Let the shadows deal with them, quietly if possible."

Jinx's brow furrowed as she concentrated. A moment later the life forces dimmed as the shadows did their work. When they finished, Daisuke could barely sense them. But he could, so that meant they were alive.

"How was that?" Jinx asked.

"Perfect. We'll deal with anyone else contemplating foolishness the same way. That's so much more efficient than using my own magic."

"Could you summon shadows of your own?" Jinx asked.

"Yes, but I don't have the same fine control over them that you do. If I wanted to send them on a rampage, that would be easy, but something like what you just did is well beyond me."

"Only because you're lazy and don't want to practice summoning and binding," Ruq said.

"You're not wrong, but if anyone's going to give me a lecture on not being lazy, it certainly won't be you. Let's move."

They set out deeper into the Sty. Nothing improved as they went from one block to the next. Oddly, nothing got much worse either. It was like the whole neighborhood was stuck in a uniform level of decay. Daisuke spotted a couple other individuals watching them pass from inside, but no one felt the need to step outside. Though if they were lookouts, whoever ran this part of the area would no doubt be getting a phone call right about now.

Jinx's face was twisted up in a disgusted look. "Is this better or worse than the last time you came here?"

"Since no one's actively trying to kill us at the moment, I'm going to say better. I had to take out three groups of the filthiest-looking men you've ever seen last time before everyone else decided they didn't need to try and rob me after all." Daisuke shook his head. "I was broke at the time. Even if they won, they would've gotten like twelve pounds."

They rounded a corner and Daisuke checked his phone. They were only two blocks from the kidnappers' home address. Where the hell was everyone? Night in the Sty was usually when things were busy. Something was very wrong.

He stopped and Jinx asked, "What is it?"

"I need to check something. Keep watch for a minute, please." Daisuke closed his eyes and sent a wave of ether out into the nearby buildings.

Just as he feared. There wasn't enough life in those buildings to say so. A few rats at most, certainly no people. As far as he could tell, the whole area was lifeless.

Jinx tugged on his shirt sleeve. "Daisuke, we've got company."

He opened his eyes to find a shambling mob of thralls headed their way, scores of them. That explained what happened to the locals. And if there were thralls, there had to be a demon binder, whether priest or wizard, around here somewhere. Daisuke put his money on the kidnappers' base.

"Do you want me to use my shadows to take them out?"

"No, they're already dead, so they have no life force to drain. We're going to have to destroy them the old-fashioned way. If you know any destructive spells, this would be a good time to use them. No need to hold back; the whole area is dead."

"And if we burn it all down, property values are bound to go through the roof," Ruq said.

Daisuke pointed and black lightning blew a path through the mob, dropping a handful of the thralls never to rise again. The rest didn't react. They just kept shambling forward like zombies. He looked closer. Were they zombies? He sensed demonic energy and assumed they were thralls, but they were even weaker and stupider than usual for thralls, so he wasn't sure. Maybe they were some fresh horror summoned just for them to play with.

He blasted another bunch of them.

Jinx did something magical and one of the whatever-they-weres collapsed, its body rotted to dust. Not a bad trick, but too slow if you had to destroy them one at a time.

Daisuke slapped his hands together, generating heat, which he expanded and compressed into a fireball. The spell streaked out and exploded, sending the monsters flying in multiple pieces. Not fire-spirit magic, but he thought he did the Kugo name proud.

A few more blasts of lightning polished off the stragglers. He blew out a breath. Those hadn't been high-tier spells, but he still felt a bit drained. Maybe that was the purpose of sending out the stupid things—wear down your opponent before fighting them yourself. That was generally all thralls were good for anyway. At least when you sent them against a competent wizard.

"Ruq, have a look around while I catch my breath. If there are more groups of thralls in the area we'll need to deal with them before we move against the main building."

"Why not just avoid them?" Jinx asked as Ruq flapped away.

"Never leave an enemy force behind you, basic tactics. We

really don't want a couple dozen thralls coming up on our six in the middle of a fight."

Jinx smiled. "Where did you learn all this stuff? I doubt they teach combat tactics at even the most prestigious boarding school."

"You'd be surprised. A lot of it I picked up in history class from studying ancient battles. The rest came from the school of hard knocks. Nearly dying is a great instructor, but I can't really recommend it."

There are no more visible, Master. I did find a building surrounded by a powerful demonic aura that I'm guessing is the place we're looking for.

Can you tell the aura's effect?

Just ambient corruption as far as I can tell at a glance. After what you've dealt with fighting Vorgon, it shouldn't be an issue. At least assuming the fight doesn't last hours.

Thank you, that's very reassuring. Stay where you are. Jinx and I will be there in a moment.

"Did he find anything?" Jinx asked.

"You can tell I was speaking with Ruq?"

"It's not hard. You fall silent and get a faraway look in your eye. So?"

"The outside is clear, but the building has an aura of corruption. You're half shadow demon, so it shouldn't cause you any trouble and I've got plenty of experience working in nasty places, but we won't want to screw around either. Ruq's waiting. What say we go take a look?"

Jinx nodded. "What was done in this place is a sort of evil I've never seen before. Did you notice a few of those thralls couldn't have been more than twelve years old?"

"Honestly, I tried not to look too closely. They're walking corpses. Whatever they were before is long gone. If you think about what we face too deeply, it can drive you crazy. Come on. Let's find whoever did this and send them to whatever hell is waiting to claim them."

"Yes. I don't generally like violence, but in this case, I'm very much looking forward to it."

Daisuke shivered a little. He dearly hoped to never hear Jinx talking about him in such a cold tone.

CHAPTER TEN

Daisuke's footfalls sounded more like gunshots in the silent night. He stayed a stride ahead of Jinx as they ran toward the kidnappers' base of operations, a sprawling building that looked like someone had combined four tenements into a single, huge complex. It was hideous, with soot-blackened clapboards, smashed windows, and a roof with more holes than shingles. It fit in perfectly with the Sty's aesthetic.

"Shouldn't we be sneakier?" Jinx asked.

"No point. As soon as we destroyed the thralls, whoever made them knew it. We're not taking anyone by surprise today, more's the pity."

An explosion filled the night and a section of the roof exploded upward in a gout of reddish-black flames.

Daisuke skidded to a stop.

That was hellfire, Master.

So I assumed. Get down here. I don't want us separated if there's a hellpriest running around.

"That wasn't aimed at us," Jinx said. "Why blast a hole in your own roof?"

"Why do these lunatics do anything? Nothing's changed. We still need to get in there."

There was another explosion, this one with no gout of flame. The walls trembled and bits of wood fell to the ground.

"Okay, change of plans," Daisuke said. "Our first priority is to find out if there are any kidnapping victims in there and get them out before the dump collapses."

"I can send my shadows in to search. They're intangible, so falling bits of wood won't hurt them."

"Great, do that. I'm going to take a peek through the hole in the roof and see if I can figure out who or what is trying to flatten the place. Ruq, you're on lookout duty."

"I'm always on lookout duty."

"Would you rather fly in and find out who's throwing hellfire around?"

"It was just an observation," Ruq said.

Daisuke swallowed a sigh and closed his eyes. A moment later his sight flew up over the building. Peering through the ten-foot hole in the roof, only smoke and dust was visible. A moment later a flare of hellfire flashed and vanished just as quickly, revealing nothing of any great interest.

He was about to fly in for a closer look when Jinx touched his shoulder. "They found two girls and a boy, all locked in cages but still alive. They're in the far-left corner of the building."

Far left, huh? Going through the interior was a good way to get crushed or fried. Best to find another way in.

"Master, company coming."

Company turned out to be a quartet of bedraggled

humans dressed in black robes trimmed in red runes. They staggered around, seeming not fully in control of their bodies. Or maybe they were on drugs. He had no idea and couldn't have cared less. Whoever they were, they were no threat. Of course, they might know something useful, assuming he could get it out of them.

"Could I get you to throw some shadow webs over those four? We'll question them after."

Jinx pointed and black threads wrapped the four people from head to foot and they collapsed. Daisuke used a telekinesis spell to pull them a safe distance away. That done, he set out for the left rear corner of the building.

The trip didn't take long and a good thing too. The blasts and explosions continued steadily. A section of the roof had fallen in, and it looked like only good luck was holding the rest of it up.

Jinx pointed at a section of blank wall. "My shadow is directly beyond that wall. There's a hall lined with cages where the students are being held."

Daisuke drew a door shape with his index finger then snapped his fingers. Necrotic energy reduced the already half-rotten wood to sawdust. He conjured a light and stepped through the opening.

"Get us out of here!" a shrill female voice said. Sounded like at least one of the prisoners was energetic enough to run for it.

The other two were on their feet, though they looked like they'd gone a couple rounds in the cage. Bruises covered their faces and the guy's right eye was swollen shut.

A rumble ran through the building. Right, no time to scrutinize the victims. He cast the same spell, this time reducing the steel bars to metal filings. "Everyone out, now!"

They didn't need to be told twice. They all ran out the hole he'd made as fast as their conditions allowed. Daisuke came last and when they stopped only twenty yards away, he shooed them further along. At fifty paces they all stopped. The guy, who had been beaten the worst, dropped to the ground. Daisuke wouldn't have wanted to sit on pavement in the Sty, but considering how filthy his clothes already were, it didn't make that much difference.

"Thanks, mister," said a girl with an ugly bruise on her cheek and dried blood on her lip. "I thought we were going to die in there. Are you with the police?"

"He can't be," the shrill woman said. She looked a couple years older than the other two and didn't have a mark on her. "This is the Sty and the police don't come here. Who are you anyway?"

"A good Samaritan." Daisuke offered a friendly smile. "I stopped a couple kidnappers earlier this evening and decided to come here and see if any of their coworkers had better luck. Seems it was a good thing I did."

"What sort of lunatic takes that kind of risk for someone he doesn't even know?" the shrill woman asked.

Daisuke was spared from having to answer when the kidnappers' base gave a final shudder and collapsed.

"Good!" the man said. "I hope all those sons of bitches got crushed."

Two more explosions sent debris flying into the air. A gesture from Daisuke kept any of them from reaching the group. Hellfire blazed from the right-hand explosion and twisted vines surrounded the second. At the center of the vines was a man dressed in a robe similar to the one worn by the people Jinx caught earlier. In the center of the hellfire opening was a humanoid demon. It had red skin and rippled with muscle. Black horns jutted from its head and in the middle of its forehead was a circle with a mark in the center.

It couldn't be.

Daisuke whipped out his phone, zoomed in on the demon, and hit record. A moment later the battle resumed.

Vines rushed in to wrap up the demon only to be reduced to ash.

"The demon belongs to Abaddon," Ruq said. "I've seen similar ones in Hell. The other must be a priest of Baphomet."

"Not a high-ranking one judging by his level of corruption," Daisuke said absently as he recorded the back-and-forth battle. "The demon's a decent tier five maybe low sixth. The fight won't last long now."

"Aren't we going to do something?" Jinx asked.

He'd been so focused on what was happening below that he'd temporarily forgotten about her. "We are doing something. We're watching and protecting the victims. Hopefully those two will kill each other, though I think it's much more likely that the demon will win. Best to let the priest wear it out as much as possible before we have to fight it."

"Why don't we just run?" the shrill woman asked.

"Do you really want a demon coming up on you from behind? Better we face it head on when we know where it is and before it has a chance to recover. Just keep quiet and relax. We'll deal with it."

"It's a demon!" she shrieked. "You can't deal with it."

"I can't if you keep distracting me."

The biggest burst of hellfire so far burned away all the vines and reduced the priest to an ash outline. Just as he figured.

The demon turned and glared right at them. Daisuke

pocketed his phone, gathered ether around himself, and got ready to fight.

Unnecessarily it turned out. The demon vanished in a burst of hellfire, leaving the Sty silent.

Daisuke remained alert, but he sensed no lingering corruption. It seemed the demon truly had fled. Weird, but he wasn't about to complain.

"I've never seen a hellfire demon leave while there were still mortals around to kill," Ruq said. "Someone must have bound it to complete that specific task."

"Lucky for us. Jinx, please leave a couple shadows to guard the prisoners. We'll chaperone these unlucky folks to the edge of the Sty then come back to question them."

"They can't get away with my webs binding them," Jinx said.

"I know. The shadows are to protect the prisoners from any locals that might decide to investigate the ruckus."

"Can we go?" the shrill woman asked.

Daisuke nodded. He would be very happy to get the woman somewhere safe then never see, or more importantly hear, her again.

CHAPTER ELEVEN

After escorting the kidnap victims beyond the Sty, Daisuke led the way back to his prisoners. He'd never dealt with a cultist of Baphomet, but doubted they were any more reasonable than the cultists of Abaddon he fought at Castle Ravenclaw. Those guys had been total fanatics, eagerly leaping into battle despite clearly having no hope of victory. They fought to the last man. He would've said it was a waste, but in Daisuke's experience, the only good demon cultist was a dead one.

"You're deep in thought," Jinx said. "Want to share?"

Daisuke blew out a sigh. "Just thinking about the past and how it might impact the future."

"Come up with any answers?"

He grinned. "Considering what we're dealing with, the answer can only be badly. Did your father ever talk about Hell or the demon lords?"

Jinx shook her head. "No, Dad hated all that. He wanted to forget what he was and move on. That I'm pretty sure he never could is kind of depressing."

"I'm sure there's a great deal about being a risen demon that's depressing. Though I'm also sure having a daughter like you mitigated it a lot

She blushed a little and his grin broadened into a full-fledged smile. It didn't last as a minute later they reached the ruined building. As fun as flirting with Jinx was, it was time to get down to business.

He found the cultists lying, unharmed, right where he left them. Crimson eyes flashed from the shadows nearby. Looked like Jinx's guards were still on duty, not that he'd seen anyone around. The locals probably knew better than to come around here.

A gesture flipped the cultists on their backs. The shadow webs wrapped them from shoulders to knees, but their faces were visible. All four looked to be either Daisuke's age or younger. In the case of one woman, he guessed middle teens. What the hell was someone that age doing with the Cult of Baphomet? He had no idea and in the end, her reasons didn't matter.

"Okay, kids, question and answer time. Your master is dead, burned to a crisp by a hellfire demon of some sort. No one's coming to save you. However, if you tell me what I want to know, I'll leave you for the police instead of letting the good people of the Sty deal with you themselves."

"There are no good people in the Sty," the young woman said with surprising venom.

"I'm aware of that. I was being sarcastic. So what were you clowns up to and why did you need wizards to do it?"

"Master Williamson said a wizard's life force was different than that of normal people and that if we sacrificed them to Baphomet, we could summon even more powerful demons," said the eldest, a pockmarked man of about twenty-four.

Daisuke frowned at that. He'd never heard of wizards having different life force. It was possible of course. When magic was involved almost anything was possible, but you'd have thought such a thing would be common knowledge.

"And this pissed off the Cult of Abaddon why?" Daisuke looked from one to the other, waiting for an answer.

A teenage boy hesitantly said, "I overheard the master talking with his familiar. It seems the Cult of Abaddon was also interested in kidnapping wizards. I guess the idea was that we'd not only make ourselves stronger but interfere with their plans as well. Two birds with one stone."

The boy's nervous giggle was one of the more pathetic sounds Daisuke had ever heard. He moved away and Jinx said, "Doesn't seem like they know much."

"No. And I'm not sure if they're truly evil or if the cult was just a way for them to find safety in the Sty. Killing desperate people just trying to survive isn't my cup of tea. If they've actually sacrificed people to Baphomet, that's another thing altogether."

"What should we do now?"

"They cooperated, so we'll drag them out for the police to deal with. Maybe they can find some way to turn them onto a better path." When he thought of the young woman's angry, bitter expression, he held out little hope. Then again, Daisuke had been angry and bitter at that age and he turned out okay, more or less.

Whatever their fate, it wasn't his concern. Daisuke needed to get back to Zurich. He had a really bad feeling about that demon and the sooner he got those fears either confirmed or denied, the better.

Delivering the cultists to the edge of the Sty had gone off without a hitch and Daisuke soon found himself at the back door of Arcane Books and Trinkets. He really hoped he was wrong about what he saw, but that was such a dim hope he hardly gave it any consideration.

"What's got you so worked up?" Jinx asked. "The demon wasn't nearly as strong as Vorgon and you defeated him easily enough."

Defeating Vorgon had been far from easy, but he understood what she meant. "That mark on its forehead looked like a demon seal. My fear is that someone got ahold of a prison and urn and now has a powerful demon under their control. It's not the Blood of Solomon. As far as I can tell, they care nothing for demonic politics. And if it's not them, then we've got yet another player in the game. Exactly what we don't need."

He unlocked the back door and they went straight to the boss's office. When he opened her door, she was reading from the Book of Wisdom. That was convenient.

"How did it go?" the boss asked. "Please tell me you learned something useful."

"Sorry, Explorers Inc. was a bust." Daisuke gave her a full report, then pulled out his phone and found an image of the demon. "That is a seal on its head, right? I'm not going crazy?"

She took his phone and looked closer. "Certainly looks like one. The resolution isn't great, but I'll see if I can find it in the book. Knowing it belongs to Abaddon will make it easier."

The boss flipped through the book, the swish of its pages sounding especially loud in the silent office. At last she stopped and grimaced. That couldn't be good.

"Found it. It seems you had the dubious luck to run into Dostrik, a greater hellfire demon. According to this, he was the third weakest of the demons Abaddon sent to fight Solomon the Wise."

"If the Cult of Abaddon got their hands on the prison and seal, that would explain how they knew his true name and kept him from going on a rampage," Daisuke said. "A demon cult with a greater demon in their service is less than encouraging."

"All the demon cults are certainly interested in freeing and gaining control over their respective patrons' demons. That one has apparently succeeded is hardly shocking."

"I suppose. Anything from Helena?"

The boss shook her head. "She's still waiting and watching. You know how these things go. It might be days, weeks, or just hours before the target shows up. And he might not show up at all. We just have to wait and hope for the best."

"Right, wait and hope, my two favorite things."

"I thought your two favorite things were food and se—"

"Quiet, Ruq, I was being sarcastic again. Though now that you mention it, some food and a few hours' sleep would be welcome."

"Go ahead and rest," the boss said. "I'll make some calls and see what my contacts know about the Cult of Abaddon. If Helena hasn't called in by noon, you can start investigating that demon."

Daisuke nodded. "Works for me, boss. Can't say why, but my gut tells me this is going to be a tough one."

"I have no doubt you're right about that. Go on."

Daisuke took his leave. First food and sleep. He'd worry about the rest in the morning.

CHAPTER TWELVE

Twelve hours' sleep and a full stomach always put Daisuke in a good mood. At least until he remembered that he was investigating a demon cult today. It wasn't so much the job that bothered him; he investigated demon cults on a semiregular basis. That was just part of the job. No, what bothered him was the overwhelming sense that something really bad was going to happen. He had little to base the feeling on, but it had been nagging at him ever since Venice.

It was the whole selling tame demons to criminals thing. That was a new one and not a precedent he liked. The police had enough to keep them busy without worrying about running into demons. Hopefully it was a onetime thing and not a new trend.

He sighed and finally rolled out of bed. His phone said ten o'clock and there were no messages from the boss. That meant no news from Helena. She was probably ready to pull her hair out. No, that wasn't fair. She had way more patience than Daisuke. *He* would've been ready to pull his hair out for sure.

Since he didn't have to go in until noon, a leisurely breakfast would be just the thing. He wasn't sure where Jinx was on her weekly eating schedule, but hopefully she'd want to join him.

"Can't you get it delivered?" Ruq crawled up on the bed in his rat form. "That way I can eat too."

"Not a terrible idea. Is she still watching TV?"

"She was when I gave up and came in here. You'll never guess what caught her eye last night."

"Phone sex?"

"Televangelists. The last thing I saw her watching was some fat, bald human that said unless you sent him one hundred euros the world was going to end. I like a good con as much as the next demon, but this guy wasn't even putting any effort in. The worst part was, he had a real-time counter that showed how many donations were coming in. The number was depressingly high."

Daisuke shrugged and finished getting dressed. "There are a remarkable number of stupid humans in the world. Better for everyone if they spend their time and money on people like your conman than on doing real evil."

Ruq leapt from the bed to Daisuke's shoulder. "Do you know what really bothers me about the whole thing? That none of the demon cults thought of it first. It's like they're not even trying."

"Scamming people is too low on the evil scale for them. Demon cults, at least in my experience, want to summon demons and take over countries, not bilk chumps out of their hard-earned money."

He pushed the bedroom door open and stepped into the

living room. Jinx was lying on his couch sound asleep. If she needed to sleep, then hopefully she would be hungry as well.

"What should we order?" Ruq asked in a louder voice than strictly necessary.

Jinx let out a little groan and sat up. She'd slept in her clothes and now they were wrinkled and her hair was poking up at wild angles. Despite all that, she still looked stunning.

When she noticed Daisuke she scrubbed a hand across her face. "I'm sorry. I didn't mean to fall asleep on your couch."

He shrugged. "No harm done, though the bed is more comfortable. You'll have to try it some night."

She blushed, which brought a smile to his face. "I don't think I'm ready for that yet."

Daisuke expected her to say that but was disappointed all the same. "How about joining us for breakfast then?"

"I could eat a little something. Just get whatever you like and I'll have a bite."

Daisuke handed his phone to Ruq. "Order us something good."

"Now you're talking." Ruq flew over to the kitchen counter where they kept the takeout menus.

"You trust a demon to order breakfast?" Jinx asked.

"Sure. Ruq and I have very similar taste in food. You holding up okay? It's been a hectic couple days."

"It's much more exciting than huddling in a cave waiting to be found and killed. Better company too. It did wear me out a bit, which is why I dozed off."

"And here I thought the televangelist put you to sleep."

She shook her head. "It was quite fascinating watching

that man last night. Do they have actual magic or is it all talk?"

"Impossible to say on an individual basis, but I'd guess ninety-nine percent talk."

They spent most of an hour on idle chitchat, ate a wonderfully unhealthy breakfast, and set out for the shop. The late morning sun felt great as they walked across Zurich. Couples were out and about, cafés were crowded, and everything seemed right with the world. Pity the reality was so much less pleasant.

They went in the back way as usual and Daisuke knocked on the boss's office door. Of course she was there and they were immediately invited inside.

"You're a little early," the boss said.

"I wish you wouldn't say it in such a surprised tone. I'm very seldom late. Anything from Helena?"

"No, all's quiet in Paris. I did hear from one of my contacts in Budapest. There's definitely something going on with the Cult of Abaddon. Apparently there was a big brawl in the market that left a bunch of civilians dead or in the hospital with bad burns. The weird part was, one bunch of cultists was fighting another bunch, all of them followers of Abaddon."

Daisuke frowned. "The way the cults are structured doesn't usually allow for that sort of thing. The leader squashes anyone looking to make trouble before it spills over."

"Usually," the boss agreed. "But clearly not this time. Some of the survivors escaped and the local security forces are reluctant to deal with them. My contact says that if you bring them in, you can ask them whatever you want first."

"Good deal for me. Does this mysterious contact want me to bring in prisoners or bodies?"

"As long as they're dealt with she doesn't care in the least. Have you been to Budapest?"

"Unfortunately, no."

"I was pretty sure you hadn't. I've got a jet lined up to take the two of you to Hungary. It leaves as soon as you arrive. Hanna will meet you at the airport. Be on your best behavior. This is as close to an officially sanctioned action as we ever get."

"I'm always on my best behavior. Unless Jinx has any questions, I'm good to go."

"No, it seems like a straightforward task," Jinx said.

"It does, doesn't it?" Daisuke stood. "I'm curious to see how it all goes to pieces on us."

CHAPTER THIRTEEN

Helena sat on the roof of Explorers Inc. and dealt out another hand of solitaire. She hadn't really been on the stakeout that long, but it sure felt like she had. She'd checked in with the boss an hour ago to report that there was nothing to report. It sounded like Daisuke and Jinx were making at least a little progress on their end. Not that any of them had managed to spot the elusive Blaze brothers.

The boss said that if he hadn't shown up in a week, she was free to abandon the stakeout and return to Zurich. She really hoped it didn't come to that. Failure left a bad taste in her mouth.

Morning turned to afternoon and she was just thinking about going on one of her semi-regular walks to the ground floor, when an unfamiliar car pulled up. A fancy black sedan no less.

Her heart sped up. This had to be him. She could feel it.

Infusing her body with ether and strengthening her personal shield, Helena got ready.

The driver's side door opened and a tall, slim redhead in a charcoal suit got out. He looked around as if expecting to see someone.

He was about to get his wish.

Helena leapt from the roof, landed right beside him, and wrapped him in a magical binding that secured him from neck to ankles.

"Please don't kill me. It was just too good of a deal to pass up. I'll do anything the Devil Man wants to make up for it. Please." His thick Scottish accent combined with how fast he was speaking made some of the words hard to understand.

"I'm not going to kill you," Helena said. "And I don't work for the Devil Man. I'm investigating the death of Julian Pilat. Assuming you're Emile Blaze, I have a number of questions for you."

Emile's pale, handsome face crinkled in obvious confusion. "Who?"

"One of the poor, stupid saps you tricked into working for you. I found his corpse in the Australian outback buried in a shallow grave, with a valuable magical artifact in his pocket. Any of this ringing a bell?"

"Unfortunately. That was the mission that caused all this trouble. Can we talk somewhere else? We're too exposed here."

Emile had a point, but she didn't really have a good place to conduct an interview. Well, she could stuff him in the back seat of his car and drive to Zurich. It wasn't that far and certainly no one would think to look for him there.

"Sure, I know a place, though it's a ways from here. I—"

The crack of a gun followed by a bullet pinging off of the bindings she'd placed on Emile brought the discussion to an abrupt conclusion.

At the far end of the alley, a figure in a long trench coat and pointing a pistol blocked their exit. He—at least she assumed it was a he—fired twice more, once at Helena and once at Emile. Neither bullet penetrated her spells.

"Damn it! They found me. And it's all your fault."

Helena was pretty sure none of this was her fault, but this was hardly the time to discuss it. She made a circle gesture and pointed at the assassin. The bindings tried to form, but the magic shattered before it could activate.

That had never happened to her before.

Have to try something else.

She pointed and a lance of white light streaked out, hitting his gun and blowing it to bits. He shook his injured hand and shouted something in a language she didn't recognize. Though from the tone she got the impression he'd called her something unkind.

"Let's get out of here," Emile said. "That's got to be one of the Devil Man's acolytes. You can't beat him. No one can beat them."

"I'm not as weak as I look." Helena shoved Emile into the car, casting a long-duration tracing spell on him in the process. "Stay put. If anything happens to me, the binding will fade and you can run to your heart's content."

She slammed the door and turned to face the assassin. He was fumbling with something under his jacket. He finally pulled out what looked like a wooden mask and touched it to his face while mumbling something.

The mask fused to his flesh and as it did he grew taller and more muscular. His clothes were absorbed and transformed into thick red skin. Finally, black horns emerged from his skull. An uncomfortably familiar symbol decorated the demon's forehead. She didn't know which one it was, but that had to be one of Solomon's demons.

Despite her boasting to the contrary, Helena knew she was in serious trouble.

The demon roared and hurled reddish-black flames at her.

Helena dove out of the way, her skin tingling from the near miss.

She rolled to her feet and countered with a barrage of golden arrows. The spell shattered on the demon's skin without effect.

Yes, she was definitely in trouble.

The demon charged.

Helena sprinted for the storefront, slammed through the closed door and ran up the stairs. At the top she spun and blasted the demon with a golden ray as it started to pursue. As with the golden arrows, this spell was totally ineffective.

The demon took the stairs three at a time.

She tried to run.

It lunged, grabbed her ankle, and sent her sprawling to the ground.

Helena rolled over just in time to watch a fist the size of her face descending toward her head.

Velcan touched his face and concentrated with all his might as he pictured his feeble human form. It took everything he had, but at last the demon mask peeled away and he was human again. His body trembled and his hand shook as he slipped the mask back into the special slot in his jacket.

He looked down at the unconscious wizard. He'd held

back enough to be sure not to kill her. Wizards were a valuable commodity, especially for the Cult of Abaddon.

She'd put up a better fight than he expected. Lasted long enough for Emile to escape anyway. The master wasn't going to be pleased with that, but Velcan hoped he'd accept the wizard's capture as a partial success.

Velcan sat on the stairs before he fell. Using the mask always took a lot out of him and he'd only been assigned the weakest of Abaddon's demons as his partner. He didn't know how Nicholas managed with Dostrik. He figured teaming up with an even more powerful demon would kill him after a single merging.

He scrubbed a hand across his face and dug out his phone. He tapped the only number in it and a moment later a gruff voice asked, "What news, Velcan?"

"I found Emile, but there was a wizard attempting to capture him as well. We fought and I defeated her, but Emile escaped in the process. Send a team to help me load her. We're at the store. She's pretty strong and will make a good sacrifice when we're ready to summon the next demon."

"On our way. Will you alert the master?"

There was only one answer to that question. "Yes. He's my next call."

Velcan hung up and pocketed the phone. Calling his master was just a euphemism. The process was a good deal more complicated than dialing a number. It wasn't like Castle Ravenclaw had cell service after all.

From a different pocket Velcan pulled out a clear crystal sphere the size of his fist. He closed his eyes and pictured a river of hellfire. This was the activation image. Soon the crystal grew warm in his hand. Should anyone other than a worshipper of Abaddon try to use the crystal, it would explode and hellfire would consume the offender.

Of course, Velcan had nothing to worry about. His faith was strong and soon the master's shadowy form appeared in the crystal's depth. He wore a hooded cloak that obscured his appearance at all times. No one knew what he really looked like or even what his name was. They all called him master. The rest of the world knew him as the Devil Man.

"You failed," the master said.

"Yes, Master." Velcan knew better than to try and make excuses. Few things angered the master more than that. "I have taken a powerful wizard prisoner. She was after Emile as well. I would've had him if she hadn't interfered."

"For ordinary humans, the Blaze brothers are proving most difficult, but no matter. Nicholas is on his way to Paris. He will take over the search. Bring the woman to me. If she's as strong as you say, then her and the other one will be enough to complete the spell. Assuming Nicholas succeeds."

Velcan winced at being removed from the hunt, but complaints were as unwelcome as excuses. "Understood, Master. I will bring her to the castle directly."

"Good. We're on the brink of the birth of a new world, Velcan. I can feel it."

He never knew what to say when the master spoke of such things. Velcan was a simple man at heart. His whole life he'd been weak. Trading his soul for power had not been a difficult choice. But it also didn't make him a visionary.

That, of course, was why Velcan was a servant and not the master.

CHAPTER FOURTEEN

The jet that carried Daisuke and Jinx to Budapest was a far cry from the Puddle Duck, the ancient cargo plane he and Helena had flown to Australia on. Sleek and state of the art, it had leather seats, a free bar that he didn't explore, and a cute stewardess. Better yet, they didn't have to jump out of it and fly to the ground. He had no idea how the boss scored this fine transport, but he had no intention of complaining.

He glanced at Jinx who was staring out at the clouds with a rapt expression.

"First time flying in a plane?"

She jumped as if surprised to hear him speak then dragged her gaze away from the window. "Yes. The clouds and sky are so pretty from up here. Have you flown many times?"

"I don't know what you consider many, but this is maybe my tenth flight and my first in a plane this nice. The boss went all out for our trip. I have no idea who she had to bribe to get us such a sweet ride, but I'm grateful."

"Me too. When I agreed to join your group, I expected danger, but the new sights and experiences have been more than worth the risks."

"I'm glad you're enjoying it. For my part, I'm usually so focused on the task at hand, I forget to enjoy the view as it were."

This was where Ruq would usually interject some rude comment, but the imp had strict instructions to stay silent and invisible on the plane. The boss gave the order in her sternest voice so even Daisuke didn't dare crack a joke.

"Coming up on Budapest International Airport," the pilot said over the speaker. "Buckle yourselves in, we'll be landing in a few minutes."

The seatbelts were an unnecessary precaution for two magic users, but Daisuke clicked his into place anyway. Jinx's snapped into its slot a moment later.

The plane slowly descended until the tires hit the tarmac with a shrill squeal. Then it was just a matter of the pilot steering them to the point of disembarkation. Hopefully, Hanna would be there waiting. The flight had been a nice interlude, but he was eager to get back to the hunt. Whatever was going on with the Cult of Abaddon had him worried, more worried than usual anyway. No doubt that was a lingering sentiment from learning Castle Ravenclaw was involved.

The plane stopped and the stewardess hurried past them. She stood beside the door and smiled as they approached. The steps had been lowered from the outside. "Thank you for flying with us. I hope you enjoy your time in Budapest."

Daisuke smiled back, keeping his gaze from wandering down to her too-tight blouse by sheer force of will. "Thank you for the smooth flight. Should we need to fly again, I hope it will be on your plane."

He led the way down the steps and spotted a woman in a gray uniform standing beside an official-looking, but unmarked SUV. That had to be Hanna. When Jinx made it down the steps, he led the way to where she was parked.

"Daisuke Kugo?" she asked.

"Yup. The pretty lady beside me is Jinx. That would make you Hanna, the boss's friend." He held out his hand.

"Correct," she said.

As they shook he gave Hanna a closer look. He put her age at about forty, if the lines around her eyes and lips were any indication. She wore no makeup and her dark eyes had a hard edge. She filled out her uniform nicely, but there was no sign of anything soft about her. All in all she gave the impression of a woman not to be trifled with.

When Jinx released her hand Hanna said, "Climb in. We'll talk as we drive. Our agents have eyes on what we believe is a Cult of Abaddon safe house and my superiors want them dealt with as quickly as possible."

Daisuke climbed into the front seat and Jinx took the back. Hanna got behind the wheel and started driving. No one gave them any trouble as they left the airport and merged onto the highway.

"So what happened?" he asked.

"A battle broke out in the central market. Both sides were hurling hellfire around without a care for who they hit. A dozen stalls were destroyed and two fixed shops burned to the ground. Three civilians dead and twenty sent to the hospital with burns that can't be healed with modern medicine. There's a priest there now praying over them." Hanna gave a shake of her head as if not quite believing what she just said.

"Healing isn't my specialty," Daisuke said. "But I might be able to do something to help them. Would you like me to take a look?"

Hanna's hard expression cracked into a faint smile. "It's kind of you to offer, but you're not here, at least not officially. The fewer people you have contact with, the better."

He nodded, disappointed but not surprised. "What happened to the cultists?"

"The larger group wiped out the smaller one then the survivors fled into the city. We're trying to identify the dead ones, but hellfire doesn't leave much behind. The only reason we know where they ended up was a tip called in by a witness. It's been two days, but no one has left the building. A delivery of fresh food arrived this morning, but other than that, no one has come or gone."

"Licking their wounds and planning their next move, I'll bet. Hopefully we can hit them before they're fully recovered. Fighting weakened demon cultists is always preferable to fighting healthy ones."

"Are you not the honorable warrior type that only likes a fair fight?" Hanna asked.

Daisuke snorted at that. "Just because I'm Japanese doesn't mean I'm some kind of wannabe samurai. The only good fight is one you win. The details don't mean a damn thing as far as I'm concerned. If I have to fight, I take out my opponents without mercy or thoughts of honor."

"That's a bit harsh," Hanna said. "Good. You looked so young, I wanted to make sure I wasn't dealing with an idealist. These monsters don't deserve mercy. I don't care what you have to do, just as long as no one save the two of you emerge from the building alive."

With an attitude like that, Daisuke was pretty sure Hanna wasn't a member of the city police force. More likely she was part of the intelligence apparatus. He'd dealt with a few spooks over the years and they all had attitudes similar to hers. He appreciated it as it made his work vastly easier.

Hanna pulled off the highway and turned into what looked to him like a respectable, middle-class part of the city. The area was dominated by low-rise apartment buildings that were well maintained. There were also shops, laundries, restaurants, and other businesses.

She pulled into a parking lot and when they stopped, everyone got out. Daisuke glanced around, but saw nothing that screamed "demon cult in the area."

"Where are they?" he asked.

"Two blocks north. I wanted to approach on foot just to be safe. My people are set up on the roof of a building across the street. We can get a report then you can decide how you want to enter the building. It won't be easy. From what I've seen there are no concealed avenues of approach."

"One of the good things about magic is that you can often make your own concealment. Please, lead the way. I'm eager to get this done."

A brief conversation with the grim men on duty across from the cult hideout gave Daisuke a pretty good idea what he was dealing with. From the sounds of it the survivors weren't in great shape. Pity for them demon magic wasn't much good for healing. Assuming, of course, they didn't have a bunch of prisoners in there whose life force they could drain. Since several days had passed with no sign of movement, he felt confident that they didn't.

He and Jinx stood alone on the bottom floor of the stakeout building. Hanna had remained on the roof with the lookouts. That was just as well, since he didn't want her anywhere near when the fighting broke out. Non-wizards were nothing but a liability in a magical battle.

"What do you think?" Jinx asked.

"I think it would be nice to have a map of the building. It's only three stories and Hanna says there's no basement, so it shouldn't be too hard to sweep. I figure we turn invisible, cross the street, and sneak in the back door. After that, it's just a matter of hunting the cultists down and eliminating them. I would like to take one of them alive for questioning if possible. Can I leave that to you?"

She nodded. "Unless they're exceptionally strong, my shadow webs will hold them. The only problem I can see is that I can't turn invisible."

"You can merge with my shadow."

Jinx started taking her clothes off without comment.

"What about me?" Ruq asked. The imp was still invisible, but with no one else around, it was safe for them to talk.

"Stay invisible. If you see a chance to take someone out, do it. But no unnecessary risks. We don't know what sort of power levels we're dealing with here."

"All set." Jinx was down to her skimpy shadow-silk dress.

Much as he would've liked to linger and enjoy the view, this wasn't the time. "Great, let's do this."

She vanished into his shadow and Daisuke wrapped himself in an invisibility spell. He retreated to the rear of the building and slipped out the side door. Next it was a quick run across the empty street. He wasn't sure if the security forces had cleared the area or if this was a naturally quiet part of the city. Probably the former. They wouldn't want anyone getting caught up in the fight.

He reached the target building's back door without issue. Unfortunately, it was locked tight. Not difficult to bypass, but a spell might draw the cultists' notice.

Daisuke shook his head. He was no locksmith. If they were going to get in, it was magic or kicking the door down, neither of which would be subtle. In that case, magic was the more certain option. Weaving a spell with careful, subtle movements, Daisuke sent a trickle of ether into the lock and rusted it to nothing.

A nudge with his knee pushed the door open. The hinges were blessedly quiet.

He paused and listened for a reaction.

No sign that he'd been noticed. So far so good.

"Jinx, you can come out now," he whispered. When she appeared beside him Daisuke asked, "Can you summon a few shadows and have them look around? They're more apt to avoid detection than we are."

Jinx nodded and crimson eyes soon appeared only to vanish again just as quickly. While the shadows scouted around, Daisuke took a quick look at their surroundings. The back door led to a kitchen that had been stripped of anything valuable. Only the sink and a refrigerator that lacked a door made it clear what the room used to be. Maybe this had been a restaurant once upon a time.

His musings were cut off by an explosion upstairs.

"They spotted my shadows," Jinx said. "There are three cultists on the second floor. They didn't make it to the third."

"No need to be subtle now." Daisuke blew a hole in the ceiling and leapt up through it.

He landed on the floor in an empty bedroom. Another explosion sounded not far away.

A couple of quick spells enhanced his standard array of defensive magic and he yanked the door open. Directly across from him a startled young man with a massive burn scar covering half his face gaped in surprise.

It was the last mistake he would ever make.

Daisuke hit him in the chest with a bolt of black lightning. The spell hurled him back into the room from which he'd begun to emerge. He sensed no life but just to be sure Daisuke said, "Check him."

Leaving Ruq to confirm the kill, Daisuke hurried toward the life forces he sensed deeper into the building.

A figure in a black robe appeared at the end of the hall and hurled a blast of hellfire at Daisuke.

A slash of Daisuke's hand conjured a wedge of dense ether that parted the hellfire on either side of him. When it had passed, he said, "Jinx! He's yours. We need him alive if at all possible."

Trusting the beautiful half demon to capture the cultist, Daisuke ran the opposite way. He sensed one more life force, but it was weak. Even worse, he sensed nothing from the top floor. Some sort of ward blocked all his magical perception. He had a sick feeling about it, but it would have to wait until they finished with this floor.

He rounded a corner and kept going until he reached a closed door. The last life force was behind it.

A gesture sent normal lightning into the door, blowing it to bits. He strode through, ready for a fight. Instead, he found a woman with burns over half her body struggling to breathe as she wheezed on a mattress someone had tossed on the floor. She stared at him with her remaining eye. It was a look begging for mercy. Perhaps begging for death would be more accurate.

He could grant that wish.

"Can you speak?" Daisuke asked.

Her mouth moved but no sound emerged. Her lips were a charred mess and she had likely breathed in some hellfire during the battle. That would explain the wheeze and inability to breathe. He shook his head. What a horrible way to die.

He wrapped a tentacle of ether around her heart and squeezed. She shuddered and went still. The woman had made no effort to defend herself. Assuming she was a priestess, she should've been able to offer some resistance. That basically confirmed his assumption that she wanted to die.

"The other one's dead, Master." Ruq shimmered into view. "I took a quick look around his room but found nothing of interest."

"Good work. This room doesn't look very promising either. Hopefully Jinx's target won't put up too much of a fight. I want to get some answers and he's our best bet."

"What about upstairs?" Ruq asked. "You sensed the ward, right?"

He nodded. "That's our next stop."

CHAPTER FIFTEEN

Jinx hid around the corner of a hall as another gout of hellfire roared past. The heat of its passing made her break out in a sweat. She'd been chasing the cultist in black for what seemed like a long time but was probably less than a minute. Daisuke wanted him alive, but that was looking like a dim prospect.

Twice she'd tried wrapping him up in shadow webs and both times some sort of protective spell flared to life and burned them to nothing. The shadows she'd set to drain his strength had fared little better. She had yet to try any of her stronger abilities as she feared they'd be likely to kill him. She'd assumed that he'd eventually run out of strength. Conjuring that much hellfire had to be taking a toll on his mind and body, but so far every time she tried to close in, he found the strength to summon more.

It was a standoff at the moment.

What she couldn't figure out was why the repeated blasts of hellfire hadn't set the building alight. Maybe hellfire worked differently. Jinx was far from an expert on this stuff despite being half demon herself.

The latest barrage ended and she darted out. The cultist was doubled over panting for breath.

With a wave of her hand, she sent shadow webs flying out at him. The barrier flared to life, burning them away.

He hit his knees and glared up at her, his pale skin bloodless and his features twisted in impotent rage.

"Please surrender," Jinx said. "I don't want to hurt you if I don't have to."

He sneered. "And submit to questioning or the tender mercies offered by a whore of Astaroth? I think not. Better to face Abaddon's wrath for my failure."

Before she could react, the cultist glowed red and exploded in a burst of blood and hellfire. Only a hastily conjured shadow barrier kept her from getting scorched.

What sort of person could do that to themselves? She hated to think about it. Even worse, Daisuke would be disappointed in her failure.

Jinx sighed. No sense putting it off. She concentrated and soon sensed him in the opposite direction but not that far off. She turned and trudged away, leaving the gory mess behind. To save energy, she also banished her shadows. Maintaining them was only a modest drain on her, but better to save as much as she could. Somehow, she doubted their day was done.

A couple turns later she found Daisuke, with Ruq perched on his shoulder in his demon form, standing in front of a set of stairs leading to the third floor. Jinx sensed the magic up there, but she couldn't tell exactly what it did.

When she was only a few feet away Daisuke turned to face her. "Did you get him?"

Jinx shook her head and told him what happened. "He just blew himself up. I mean, who does that?"

"Demon cults tend not to attract the most mentally stable people in the first place. A suicide hellfire bomb is hardly outside the realm of possibility. It's a shame we won't get to question him, but he is eliminated and you're safe. All in all, not the worst result. Hopefully we can find something useful upstairs."

Jinx let out a quiet sigh. He wasn't mad. "Can you tell what the magic does?"

"I've been analyzing it. There's an anti-fire component, probably to prevent the building from burning down when they're training. There's also a weak aura of corruption that makes wielders of demon magic stronger and holy magic users weaker. That's a pitiful thing compared to some I've seen. The problem is, I'm not sure if there's anything else. I think that's it and I'm sure there's nothing offensive in the mix. I was just debating taking a look when you showed up. Can you tell anything about it?"

Jinx peered at the ether, but it was too complex a spell for her. The things she did were innate abilities, magic she was born able to do. She was no wizard trained in the use of spells.

"Sorry, I can't make heads or tails of it."

"That's fine. I just figured having a second set of eyes look things over would be prudent."

"Third set!" Ruq said.

Daisuke grinned. "Right, third set. Pity it seems we've learned all we can from down here. It's time to take a look upstairs."

"I'm ready," Jinx said. She wasn't sure that was completely true, but she was game nonetheless.

"Actually, I was hoping you'd wait down here."

"Why? I won't get in your way."

"I have no doubt of that, but when investigating something like this, if you have the option, it's best to leave someone in the safe zone. Should something happen to me, you can either rescue me yourself, or get help should you deem it necessary. If we both get taken out, we're screwed."

Jinx chewed her lip. What he said made sense, but it still felt like she was being left out. But she was very much the junior partner in this team so at last she nodded. "Okay. If anything happens, I'll get you out for sure."

He squeezed her shoulder. "Never doubted it."

Jinx wasn't sure who a half demon should pray to, but wished with all her might that nothing would happen to Daisuke. She didn't know what she'd do if she lost him.

Daisuke took a deep breath and put his foot on the bottom step. No reaction from the wards. That pretty much confirmed his theory that there was nothing offensive in the spell. He felt the corruption, but it was nothing compared with Vorgon's aura. He had no intention of lingering, but even if he needed a few hours, he doubted it would be a problem.

Content that his initial analysis had been correct, Daisuke quickly climbed the rest of the stairs and pushed the door at the top open. A light burst to life at his mental command, revealing a single huge room that took up the entire top floor. In the center an arcane symbol had been drawn in white chalk. Five bloodred candles burned with hellfire at the major intersections. In the very center of the symbol sat a black book.

Looking away from the symbol, he studied the rest of the space. Not that there was much to see. Chains hung from the ceiling on the left-hand wall, but there were thankfully no people shackled to them at the moment.

"You know more about Abaddon than I do," Daisuke said. "Any thoughts?"

"It looks like a pretty standard summoning chamber," Ruq said. "A lot of people make the mistake of thinking their only purpose is to bring demons to this world, but you can also summon demonic energy or make offerings to your patron."

"I imagine that's what the chains are there for."

"That's right. Abaddon not only likes having people burned alive for his glory, but he also savors the fear and despair of those watching and waiting their turn in the flames."

"Charming. Dealing with the spell circle should be simple enough, don't you think? Snuff the candles first, then erase a few lines and we should be good to go."

"Agreed, but that book looks interesting. That might be a worship journal. Lots of good information in there I'll bet."

Daisuke frowned. "I've never heard of such a thing."

"Really? Some cultists use them as a way to show their devotion to their patron. Basically they write down everything they've done to further their master's vision and then pray over it in the hopes that Abaddon or whoever will see what they've accomplished. No idea if any of the demon lords actually look at them, but I'm pretty sure that's what the book is."

"Huh. You learn something new every day. I'll wrap it in a

protective bubble before I get started. Wouldn't do to lose our last chance at some useful intel."

Daisuke raised his hands and paused. This might end up being trickier than he expected. He pulled the metal card out of his pocket and summoned his trunk. The Staff of Law wouldn't be a huge help in this situation, but any extra power could only be a good thing.

He returned the trunk to its pocket dimension and raised the black staff. Ether gathered and he got to work. First a thick bubble formed around the book. Next he examined the candles. There was no obvious indication of a proper order to extinguish them. Just to be on the safe side, he snuffed them all out at the same instant.

No reaction from the circle. So far so good.

Now the trickier bit. He pointed the staff at the widest line in the circle and blasted it with concentrated ether. It resisted for a moment then a gap formed.

Black sparks shot up as the magical flow was interrupted.

He quickly severed two more lines.

The sparks exploded up in a pillar of darkness that blew a hole in the roof. When the darkness faded, the circle was gone and the book remained unharmed. The oppressive feeling that had hung over the building was gone as well.

"I think we're done here."

"I can't sense any more magic," Ruq agreed. "That was a more violent reaction than I was expecting. I doubted these losers had the power to create a summoning circle that strong."

"We don't know how long they've been working on it." Daisuke retrieved the book and put both it and the staff in his trunk. "Come on. I've had enough of this place."

They climbed down the stairs and found an anxious Jinx waiting. "Are you okay?" she asked.

"Yeah, no problem." He told her what they found. "Let's keep the book to ourselves for now. If there's anything useful, the boss can pass it along to Hanna."

"Is that okay?" Jinx asked.

Daisuke shrugged. "We did all the work. How hard can she complain?"

He led the way down to the front door and strode right out. Before he could make it across the street Hanna and her team were emerging from the building that served as their watch post.

"Is it done?" Hanna asked.

"Other than the cleanup. You'll find three bodies inside, one of which exploded."

"Do I want to know how that happened?" Hanna asked.

"We didn't do it," Daisuke said. "It was a suicide hellfire bomb. He tried to take Jinx to meet Abaddon with him but happily failed. Do you need a detailed report or anything?"

"As long as the cultists are dead and the magic neutralized, you're good to go. It's not like the two of you answer to me. Though speaking of that, you're not looking for a new job by any chance? I could use agents like you two."

Daisuke laughed. "I think we'll stick with our current employer. It was nice meeting you, Hanna. Though I wish the circumstances had been more pleasant."

"You and me both. If you ever visit Budapest for pleasure, look me up. I'll treat you to dinner."

Daisuke grinned. "You're on."

She led her team into the building and Daisuke turned to find Jinx frowning at him. "You were flirting with her."

"Yes. It's my natural way of acting with women. Relax, she's not really my type. A little too old and way too serious."

"What about having dinner with her?"

He nearly laughed again before he realized she was serious. "I don't expect to be in Budapest again anytime soon. And even if I am, dinner with Hanna would be just that, dinner. Nothing more."

His phone rang, ending the awkward conversation. "Yeah, boss."

"Are you finished there?" the boss's voice was tight with tension.

"We just wrapped things up. What's happening?"

"Helena missed her first contact window." Daisuke's heart skipped a beat. "Technically she won't be overdue for another twelve hours, but I'd feel better if you went to check on her. The jet's ready to take you to Paris."

"Forget that. I've been to Paris plenty of times. Text me the address and I'll be there in a blink."

"It's probably nothing, but better safe than sorry. Address incoming. Contact me as soon as you confirm she's okay."

"Will do." He hung up and a few seconds later a text appeared with a Paris address.

"Everything okay?" Jinx asked.

"No. Helena missed her first call-in window. It might be serious or it might be nothing, but either way, we're going to find out right now."

CHAPTER SIXTEEN

Helena's head bounced off something hard, jarring her awake. She opened her eyes but found the world every bit as dark as before. Grimacing, she went to rub her eyes only to find that her hands were bound behind her back. Her legs were also tied up at the ankle.

She cudgeled her brain, trying her best to remember what happened and how she ended up wherever she was. It didn't take long for everything to come rushing back. The demon, Emile Blaze, all of it. Now that she remembered, she couldn't help wondering why she was still alive. When the demon's fist came crashing down at her head, she'd figured that was the end.

Waking up in the dark with a throbbing headache now seemed like a gift rather than a punishment. For the life of her, Helena couldn't imagine why the demon hadn't killed her. It was a very non-demon thing to do, not that she planned to complain.

The question now was, where in the world had she ended up? With her luck, those two kidnappers she ran off returned to collect her unconscious body and she was on her way to some underground slave market. Who was she kidding? Escaping those two would be a cinch. She should be so fortunate as to end up with them as her captors.

Maybe a little light would reveal more about her situation. She concentrated and tried to call on her magic, but nothing happened. When she tried to focus, her mind spun and she couldn't get the ether to react. Without access to her magic, the situation became a lot bleaker.

Another thud and her head bounced off the hard floor. She was pretty sure she was in the back of a moving car. How long she had been here was another question and one she couldn't begin to answer. She could be hundreds of miles away from Paris at this point. How would Daisuke ever find her? If the demon left some of her blood behind, he could use a tracking spell. But that was a big if.

Well, it wasn't like he was the one without access to his magic. There were plenty of options available to him. Helena had full faith that Daisuke would find her. She just hoped it would be in time.

Sometime later it felt like the car slowed then stopped. A door slammed and she tensed as footsteps crunched closer. It seemed she was about to find out who grabbed her.

The trunk squeaked open and she squinted against the light. All Helena could see of her captor was a dark silhouette.

"Where are you taking me?" She intended for the question to sound demanding but the words came out far too weak and trembly.

"To the master. He will be most pleased to add another strong wizard to his collection. I have water if you'd like a drink."

Helena frowned. A polite kidnapper was the last thing she expected. Even if she couldn't escape, maybe she could get some information out of this putz.

"A drink would be nice, thank you."

He reached in, grabbed the front of her shirt, and pulled her into a sitting position. It was done in a very businesslike fashion. No effort was wasted trying to feel her up. Helena immediately moved seduction lower on her list of tricks to attempt.

Her captor bent down and came up with a bottle of water. As he unscrewed the cap she asked, "Who's your master?"

"I don't know his real name. I'm not sure anyone does. But everyone calls him the Devil Man."

The name meant nothing to Helena. When he held the bottle out to her, she drank, careful to take her time and not choke. When she stopped he pulled the bottle away.

"Thank you."

"You're welcome." He smiled and now that her eyes had adjusted she could see he was a decent-looking guy. Pale skin, brown hair, slim, almost skinny build. Not that she could tell much considering the baggy brown clothes he wore.

"You're much nicer than the other lady wizard. Every time I offered her a drink she snarled and swore at me like a feral cat. I suppose I can't blame her given the circumstances. Still, this is much nicer. As long as you behave yourself, I'll stop regularly so you can eat, drink, and, you know. It'll have to be on the side of the road though. We can't exactly visit a rest area."

"Could you tell me about the other wizard?" Helena asked.

He checked his watch. "I guess it wouldn't hurt to talk for a couple minutes. I don't know her name. She was pretty, but not like you. Her hair was black and her skin almost copper colored. And could she ever swear. I never heard a lady swear like that."

Helena smiled at his description. She didn't mean to. It was just a natural reaction. "Sounds unpleasant."

"Oh, she was. I only stopped often enough to make sure she didn't die of heatstroke in the trunk. The master would not be happy if I brought him a corpse instead of a living sacrifice. You'll get to meet her soon. I suspect you'll be sharing a cell. Maybe she'll be nicer to a fellow lady wizard. Though I wouldn't count on it. We need to get going."

He lowered her back into the trunk, surprising her with his gentleness, then slammed the lid. Alone in the dark once more, Helena's mind raced. Not that it took her anywhere. Bound and trapped as she was, with no magic, there was no chance of escape.

In the end, her mind focused on one phrase he used, living sacrifice. That was likely to be her fate as well.

"Please, Daisuke, find me in time." Helena wasn't religious, but that was the first genuine prayer she'd ever offered. Only time would tell if it did her any good.

CHAPTER SEVENTEEN

Daisuke stepped out of the shadows in Paris with Jinx a step behind him. She'd put her clothes back on while he made a brief report to Hanna and now the two of them looked like any other visitors wandering around Paris. At least here, unlike London, they didn't have to worry about anyone asking about their passports. France was an open nation and people were free to come and go as they pleased.

He checked the map on his phone. Explorers Inc. was in a rough part of the city, the no-go zone where gangs mostly ran things. Weird place to set up a business, but whatever. At this point he was pretty sure there was damn little legitimate about them.

He'd chosen a location near the center of the city, which meant they had a ten-minute walk to the target neighborhood. Getting his bearings, Daisuke set out.

"Do you think she's okay?" Jinx asked. She sounded genuinely worried about her self-proclaimed rival.

"I wish I could say yes. I want to say yes, but the truth is,

Helena is far more conscientious about making her call-ins than I am. If she missed one, I can only think it's because she was physically unable to do so. I'm trying really hard not to think the worst. Helena's a skilled wizard and a tough woman. I won't believe she's dead until I see a body."

"If not that, then what?"

Daisuke shook his head. "No idea and speculating won't do us any good."

He set a brisk pace, ignoring the many sights, sounds, and smells of Paris. He felt certain that the late afternoon city was beautiful, but he had neither the time nor the inclination to enjoy it. All Daisuke could think about was Helena potentially lying hurt somewhere and needing his help. If somebody had done something to her, he swore he'd make them wish they'd never been born.

None of the happy, ignorant people they passed in the street troubled them and soon they closed in on Explorers Inc. Daisuke slowed and increased the power of his personal shield.

"Ruq, take a look, but don't do anything crazy."

No comment from the imp, which he appreciated. Daisuke opened his mind fully to the ether and found nothing in the way of life forces nearby. Not a great sign.

He also found something else, a faint trail running through the ether. It was the residue from an extended-duration tracing spell. He'd used them himself on several occasions and recognized it at once. Helena must've tagged someone. If they came up blank in the building, he at least had a direction to search next.

"Nobody home, Master," Ruq said. "There are signs of battle and I found a small patch of dried blood. Not enough to have come from a serious wound."

"Hopefully I can use it for a tracking spell. Wherever Helena might be, it certainly isn't here."

"Daisuke, look." Jinx had moved to the far end of the side street.

He went to join her and she handed him some spent cartridges. "Who'd be dumb enough to try and use a gun on a wizard?"

"Maybe they don't have anything to do with Helena," Jinx said. "I imagine there are plenty of shootings around here."

Daisuke eyed the brass and shook his head. "These are fresh, not a bit of corrosion on them. I doubt they've even been here for a day. Good job finding them. I was so focused on magic I didn't even think to look for something ordinary."

She offered a gentle smile. "Just doing what I can. Did you find anything?"

"Ruq found a small patch of blood. I'm going to see if there's enough for a tracking spell. Will you keep watch out here?"

"Sure, no problem. Want me to detain anyone that shows up?"

"Only if they give you a reason to. I won't be long."

He retraced his steps and went into the building. The door had been smashed open. There wasn't much inside, but the floor had been gouged by what he guessed were claws. Whatever Helena fought, it wasn't human.

At the top of a flight of steps he found a reddish-brown stain. No liquid blood; that was a problem. Daisuke wasn't even sure if the spell would work if the blood had dried and soaked into the wood.

Using an ethereal gouge, he scraped out a chunk. "Okay, Helena, let's see if I can find you."

Ether wove through the wood, trying, and failing, to

establish a resonant connection. He kept at it, but after five minutes Daisuke tossed the wood aside. It was useless.

That left him one avenue to explore. He'd follow the tracing spell and see who was waiting at the other end. Hopefully they could tell him where to find Helena.

But first he needed to report in.

He dialed the shop and after a single ring the boss asked, "Did you find her?"

"No such luck. Looks like there was a fight, but she's long gone. I did find the remains of a tracing spell. I mean to follow it and see who she marked. Five'll get you ten it's a Blaze brother."

"Let's hope so. If anyone can tell us what the hell is going on, it's them. Be careful, Daisuke. Whatever or whoever took out Helena might still be in the area."

"I should be so lucky. Don't worry, I'll keep my head on a swivel."

"And keep *me* up to date. None of your lone wolf going dark bullshit. I don't have any more agents to send if you go missing."

"I'll be good, I promise. Bye, boss." He pocketed his phone.

It was time to go hunting.

Helena was half asleep when the car lurched to a stop. It hadn't been that long since Velcan let her out for a snack break, so the sudden halt came as a surprise. Maybe the car broke down and they wouldn't be able to go wherever they were going after all.

The wait was longer than usual and when she heard

crunching beside the trunk, Helena was certain there was more than one person outside. That wasn't good. The only reason she could think of was their arrival at the cult's base.

The trunk lid popped open and the light blinded her for a moment. None-too-gentle hands yanked her out.

"Easy, she was perfectly pleasant and cooperative," Velcan said. "No need to rough her up now."

"You're soft," a rough, growly voice said. "Why the master chose to give you a mask I'll never know."

Helena blinked a few more times and found herself facing a bearded man at least a foot taller than her. His massive, bare chest was covered in burn scars. One of his eyes had turned milky white but the other one glared at her with unrestrained rage. That a total stranger should draw such a strong reaction surprised Helena, but then again, perhaps he was more typical of your standard demon cultist than Velcan.

"I'm not soft, I'm polite." Velcan stood a few feet away. "I also have double your compatibility with the mask. I'm sure the master is eager to meet the new sacrifice. Let's not keep him waiting."

"I can't walk with my legs bound," Helena said.

The bigger man hoisted her over his shoulder like a sack of potatoes and they set off. All Helena could see was the gravel path and her captor's legs and ass. Not exactly the greatest view in the world. To make matters worse, his bony shoulder was driving into her stomach with each stride.

A couple minutes later the gravel changed to wooden planks as they passed over a bridge of some sort. At least that's what she assumed it was. Wood quickly turned to gravel again. She craned her head left and right, trying to get a look at where she'd ended up. A high stone wall surrounded an empty courtyard. There were no guards visible. Perhaps the cult was a small one. Of course, if you could call on demons, you didn't need many human guards.

The gravel gave way to solid stone and on either side were dark walls. Light came from magical torches set every twenty or so feet. The illusory flames gave off a warm glow but no heat. It felt like someone had gone to a lot of trouble to make this feel like a real medieval castle. Why they would go to such trouble she had no idea. Of course, when you were dealing with demon worshippers you had to throw out things like common sense.

Down halls and around corners brought them ever deeper into the castle. At least that's what she was thinking of it as until someone told her otherwise. The weird thing was that they met no other cultists. She assumed they had to be here somewhere.

At last they entered a larger room and a voice said, "Welcome home, Velcan. I see you've brought me a gift, though not the one I was hoping for. Set her down so I can have a look."

Helena let out a sigh of relief when the burly cultist set her on her feet. That relief turned out to be short lived. She was unceremoniously spun around to face an altar draped with a crimson sheet featuring a black flame in the center. Behind the altar stood a man, though she used the word loosely given his tiny horns and deep-red skin. Most of his body was hidden by a black robe embroidered with Infernal runes. If this wasn't the Devil Man, then Helena hated to think what he was going to look like.

"And who might you be, young lady?" the Devil Man said.

"Helena. Your men have been less than respectful in their

treatment of me, though as kidnappers go, Velcan seemed decent enough. What do you want with me?"

"You're going to be a guest at this castle until my agents retrieve what Emile Blaze stole from me. Then you'll be sacrificed so that I can become one with the most powerful demon in the world. When the transformation is complete, I will conquer this world in Abaddon's name!" The Devil Man raised his hands and looked to the heavens like a preacher giving a sermon.

"Let it all burn," Velcan and his fellow cultist murmured.

Helena darted a look around the room in hopes of finding something, anything, that might help her escape. What she saw was another man, this one hanging back in the shadows, but dressed in an equally black robe. His hood was raised, but she could just make out the gleam of his eyes as he watched the Devil Man.

Just another cultist. No help there. In fact, there was no help anywhere.

The Devil Man returned his attention to her. An instantaneous flash of heat severed her bonds. "Take her to the holding cells and put her in with the other sacrifice. No reason for them to spend their last days alone."

"Yes, Master," Velcan said.

"Oh, not you. Yorn can handle this on his own. You will stay and tell me everything that happened on your mission so that we might learn from your mistakes."

Velcan winced then bowed his head. "As you wish, Master."

Yorn grabbed her arm and dragged her toward the exit. Helena stumbled, trying to keep up, her tingling feet none too steady. She flicked a glance over her shoulder just before they left, but could make out nothing of what was happening.

Despite being able to see where she was going, her second trip through the dark halls was no more revelatory than her first. There were no decorations and no people. Just bare stone as far as the eye could see.

Soon enough they came to a set of stairs leading to the basement or perhaps dungeon would be more accurate. There was even less light at the bottom of the steps. A gloomy path ran between cells with iron-barred doors. The first two were empty, but the second two had guests. On the left was a man that looked like he'd been through a war. Bruises and burn marks covered his pale skin. His short red hair and scruffy beard gave Helena a clue as to who he was— one of the Blaze brothers most likely. Judging from his treatment, it was no wonder Emile was anxious not to get caught.

Yorn dragged her to the right and pulled out a heavy iron key. A woman sat huddled in the back of the cell, barely visible in the dim light. Helena caught a glimpse of dark hair, dusky skin, and red lips.

The door clanked open and Yorn shoved her through. Helena staggered but somehow kept her feet. She spun as the door slammed shut and he locked it again. Yorn stalked off without another word. Or a first word for that matter.

"Damn my luck," her roommate said. "Why did I have to get stuck with you instead of the cute Japanese boy?"

Helena knew that voice. A year had passed since she last heard it, but she recognized it all the same. "Vanessa Warhawk. Well, well. I guess I shouldn't be surprised that the Blood of Solomon was mixed up in this."

"I could say the same. Figured it was only a matter of time before the Circle of Sorcery stuck its nose where it didn't belong. Though I will admit, I never imagined us sharing a cell while awaiting sacrifice."

"Don't suppose someone from your side is coming to the rescue?" Helena asked. She wasn't entirely sure if that would be good for her or bad for her. A quick death in battle would be less painful than being sacrificed to Abaddon, but it still wasn't of any great interest to her.

"Afraid not. Solomon the Great has begun to hear the voices of the demons. He's got everyone out looking for prisons. Soon we'll have an unstoppable army."

"I like your optimism. If my boss started hearing voices, I'd be worried she was going nuts. Generous of you to think he's not losing it."

Vanessa leaned forward so the light shone off her perfect features. "You know nothing about Lord Solomon. He will bring order to this world. We should all be working together to make it happen faster, not fighting and making things worse."

"Yeah, that's going to be a no from me. I have little interest in life under the boot of a megalomaniac that thinks he's the reincarnation of the greatest wizard that ever lived. Here's a hint for you, whether it's cultists or secret societies, if the big plan involves controlling multiple demons, you're probably the bad guys."

Vanessa leaned back and rested her head on the stone wall. "Demons are just tools. Daisuke has one as a familiar after all. You don't treat him with this sort of vitriol."

"Daisuke doesn't want to rule the world and Ruq is the least demonic demon I've ever seen, putting his table manners aside. Those two have done more good than I can describe."

"If you say so."

Helena growled a little then sighed. She tried to touch the ether and failed. Maybe if she didn't eat or drink anything the drug would wear off.

"How long have you been here?"

Vanessa didn't even bother looking her way. "I don't know. Weeks, I think. The days all mush together. Only Timothy's torture sessions break up the boredom. And even those stopped when he finally told them what they wanted to know. If you're thinking of waiting the drug out, don't bother. There's something in the air down here. I only catch a whiff of it every once in a while, but I figure that's what's keeping us from using our magic. Only Yorn comes down here and he can't cast, at least as far as I can tell."

So much for that plan.

"What did they want from Timothy?"

Vanessa shifted so she was facing Helena. "The location of his brothers. Or at least his best guess. Obviously they could be anywhere."

"What, exactly, do they have that's so damned important? Everybody and his brother is looking for them and I'm still not sure what happened or why. Care to clue me in?"

Vanessa shrugged. "Guess it can't make any difference now. I sent some of their dupes after a seal, the seal for Abaddon's ace, or so our lord said. Once we had that, finding the prison would be easy. Then it would simply be a matter of research to find the elder demon's name and we'd have a most potent ally. Somehow the cult got word of the Blazes' betrayal. Three of them escaped with the seal. Timothy and I were less fortunate."

"Why not just go and get the seal yourself?"

"Ten wannabe explorers went on the retrieval mission and two made it back with the seal. That answer your question? No sense putting yourself at risk when you've got a bunch of young, eager fools to do it for you."

Helena grimaced at the blatant cowardice and self-interest. Not that she was surprised, just disgusted. If ever there was a person that deserved to be sacrificed to a demon lord, Vanessa was it. Helena just wished she didn't have to witness it up close and personal.

CHAPTER EIGHTEEN

When they'd left the rough part of Paris behind, Daisuke flagged down a cab and asked for the nearest car rental place. After a long look at Jinx, the cabbie nodded and they were on their way.

"Why do we need a car?" Jinx asked. They were speaking English in the hope that the driver wouldn't understand.

Just to be on the safe side Daisuke pitched his voice low. "Because I can't see the tracing spell from the shadow paths. I also need to concentrate, so you'll have to drive."

She didn't reply and Daisuke looked from the window to her. "You can drive, right?"

"I understand the theory, but I've never actually done it before."

He almost made a comment about sex, but thought better of it at the last minute. "It's simple enough. We'll just have to be sure to get an automatic. I can get us through the city, then you can take over."

"Is Emile not in the city?"

"Judging by the tracing spell's weakness, I'd say he's at

least a hundred miles away. That puts him way outside of Paris. My guess is he's holed up in a little country village. Probably has a cottage no one knows about. At least that's what I'd do if I wanted to hide."

"I never thought about this sort of thing before. Hiding in the outback was easy once I enchanted the locals. If those damned priests hadn't shown up, no one would've bothered us." She gave a little shake of her head. "Anyway, is this just another part of your job?"

"Pretty much, though I usually have to find things rather than people."

Ten minutes later the cab pulled up beside a lot filled with cars. "Fifteen euros."

Daisuke gave him a twenty. "Keep the change."

He and Jinx got out and went right for the office. They didn't even reach the door before a handsome man around thirty dressed in a neat suit emerged from the building. He smoothed his mustache and smiled. He looked so slick Daisuke expected to see oil dripping off of him.

"How may I help you?" he asked in slightly accented but still easily understood English.

"My girlfriend and I want to take a drive through the country. We need something comfortable with good mileage and a full tank of gas."

"I have just the thing, sir. Follow me."

The salesman set out for what would no doubt be the most expensive car on the lot.

Sure enough they ended up in front of a two-door convertible. The sleek sports car was painted cherry red with a cream interior. It was, indeed, the perfect car for a drive through the country and since Daisuke was paying with the Circle's credit card he didn't argue.

"It's perfect." He dug his wallet out. "How much for two days?"

Half an hour later they were on the road, retracing their steps to where the tracer exited the no-go zone. From there it was simply a matter of following the ethereal path. He stopped at every intersection and peered into the ether. The process was a bit herky-jerky but in the end they left Paris heading south.

Daisuke glanced at Jinx who sat trembling in her seat as she waited her turn to drive. He was doing okay on his own, so maybe this wasn't the best time for her first lesson.

"On second thought," he said. "I'll just keep going as I have been, checking at every intersection. I'll give you driving lessons sometime when there's less pressure."

"Are you sure? I'm certain I can manage, I'm just a little nervous."

"It'll be fine. If there's trouble I want you at your best, not distracted and on edge. What you can do is read that journal we found. I want to know what's going on with the Cult of Abaddon."

She visibly relaxed and said, "I can do that. I guess my education is lacking in some practical ways."

"It's a magic-user thing," Daisuke said. "For someone that's depended on magic to get around their entire life, learning to drive seems pointless. The main reason I learned was a need to move around without drawing attention. Flying everywhere isn't exactly subtle and I can only shadow walk to places I've already been. Thus the need for a car."

They reached an intersection and he checked the tracer. It turned left, onto a rough dirt road. There weren't any deep ruts or potholes visible, but if the road got any worse, he might regret getting a convertible and not a truck.

The dirt road ran through rolling hills filled with sheep pastures. It was an idyllic country setting. Daisuke could easily imagine paintings of the area being popular with apartment dwellers in the city. They passed a few farms and only two other cars. He checked all of them, but the tracer kept going straight.

"How bloody far did this clown go?" he muttered.

Jinx said nothing, her nose buried in the book.

"Considering who's after him, probably until he ran out of gas," Ruq said. The imp had shifted to his rat form and was sitting on Jinx's lap. "I bet we find him in the deepest, darkest hole you can imagine."

They topped a hill and another farmhouse appeared about a mile ahead. Daisuke checked it and grinned. "I'll take your bet. The tracer leads right to that house. Not exactly deep or dark."

Jinx looked up from the book. "I don't see a car."

"Probably in the barn out back. Hidden to make it look like no one was home."

Daisuke slowed as they got closer. The last thing he wanted was to spook Emile, assuming that was actually who Helena tagged. And he couldn't think of anyone else she'd mark with a tracer.

"How do you want to handle this?" Jinx asked as if reading his mind.

"Emile is being hunted, so he's unlikely to act rationally. We need to secure him first, then we can make it clear that we mean him no harm and hopefully get a few answers."

"Do we really mean him no harm?" Ruq asked. "We're pretty sure this guy sent a bunch of dupes out to get themselves killed, right?"

"Possibly. But if the people volunteered to go on an

adventure, we can't necessarily blame Emile for their stupidity. And it doesn't matter even if we did. We can't help the dead. All that matters now is finding Helena and learning what the Devil Man is up to. The Blaze brothers are our best and perhaps only hope of doing both. Unless Jinx found something interesting in the book."

"It is interesting, but I'm not sure if it's useful. Apparently the Devil Man returned with an outsider, a wizard, and said the way they did things was going to change. Two-thirds of the cult wanted nothing to do with an outsider joining in a leadership role. They fled and the two sides got to fighting. The wizard's magic and exactly what he did is a little vague, but it made all the difference and the larger group was nearly wiped out. The ones we fought were all that remained."

"Good to know we're dealing with a relatively small group at least. Thanks, Jinx."

He pulled into the driveway and angled the car across it. If somebody made a run for it, that would at least slow them down.

They got out of the car and Ruq shook his head. "There's no way we're getting the deposit back on that rental. Something bad always happens to the car on these missions."

Daisuke frowned. "I don't think that's right. We didn't destroy a car in Australia."

"We didn't have a car in Australia. The hatchback in Japan was totaled."

"That wasn't my fault. Natsumi was driving at the time. Anyway, get up on the roof and let me know if anyone tries to make a break for it. Remember, we need them alive, so no poison."

"I never get to have any fun." Ruq changed into a raven and flew up onto the farmhouse roof.

"You two are very lighthearted about this," Jinx said.

"Not really. The banter helps me stay relaxed. You don't want to go into a fight tense. It slows you down. A few shadows to cover the other exits would be great."

Her brow furrowed and she said, "They're in place."

"You're getting faster."

"I've had a lot of practice."

"Stick with me and you'll get a lot more." Daisuke climbed the three steps up to the porch and knocked on the front door. "Hello! Our car ran out of gas and we don't have cell service! Can we use your phone?"

Only silence answered him.

Three men just ran out the back door headed for the barn.

"We've got runners. Jinx, your shadows are up."

Daisuke left her to it and sprinted for the rear of the house. He rounded the corner of the wrap-around porch and found three redheaded men facing off with four crimson-eyed shadows that stood between them and the barn. Daisuke sensed no magic, which meant they had no hope of beating the shadows.

"Excuse me," Daisuke said. "My colleague and I need some information. We don't work for the Devil Man and we wish you no harm. I assume you're the Blaze brothers. An awful lot of people are looking for you three. Wait, shouldn't there be four of you?"

All three brothers glared at Daisuke. Maybe they were trying to be intimidating. If so, they were doing a poor job of it. Having stared down demons, the businessmen didn't frighten Daisuke in the least.

"How about we go back inside and talk things over like sensible people?"

"How about you let us be on our way?" one of the

brothers said. "You have no authority to hold us like this. It's kidnapping."

Daisuke moved closer so they wouldn't have to keep shouting at each other. "You know, authority's a funny thing. It comes in all sorts of flavors. There's the official kind that includes a badge. And the unofficial kind that comes with the ability to hurl spells capable of reducing you to a pile of smoking, rotten flesh in the blink of an eye."

He made a fist and black lightning danced around it while the shadows moved menacingly closer.

"Now, do you boys want to discuss the semantics of authority further or do you want to have a polite conversation?"

"Let's just get it over with," one of the other brothers said.

"That's exactly the attitude I like." Daisuke nodded toward the door. "Let's go inside."

They returned to the farmhouse and settled around an oval dining room table. The chairs were hard and Daisuke wouldn't have been surprised if they predated World War Three.

"Let's start with a simple one," Daisuke said. "Which one of you is Emile?"

The one that suggested getting it over with raised a hand. "I'm Emile. I assume that you're associated with the young lady that nearly captured me yesterday."

"You assume correctly. What happened to her?"

"She fought a demon, and, I further assume, lost. I can't say for sure, but the binding magic she used on me vanished and I took off like a rocket."

Daisuke kept his anger tightly under control. Whoever sent that demon was going to regret it. "Describe the demon and tell me exactly what happened."

Emile did so. The demon he described was similar to the one they saw in London, but there were enough differences to convince him that this was a different monster. That meant their enemies had at least two of Abaddon's demons under their control. What he couldn't figure out was this business with the masks. Did someone figure out how to bond the seals with masks so the demons could be controlled? That seemed impossible, but given the facts available he could think of nothing else.

"Alright, now, why does the Cult of Abaddon want you lot so badly?"

No one spoke. He tried to look each brother in the eye, but no one could meet his gaze. That was seldom a good sign.

At last Emile said, "When we were trying to set up Explorers Inc., no one would loan us the money we needed. We started looking for less...traditional methods of financing. Word must have reached the Devil Man as a lawyer showed up one day and offered us all the money we needed with the caveat that we had to send our explorers looking for specific artifacts and that those items had to be turned over to him, the lawyer that is. At this point we knew nothing about the Devil Man. We were free to keep anything else we found. The artifacts would also serve as the loan repayment, so we wouldn't need to make any other cash payments."

"Sweet deal," Daisuke said. "Maybe a little too sweet. How much did you get?"

"Five million. In hindsight it was too good to be true." Emile sighed. "But when someone dangles your dream right in front of your nose, it's really hard to say no."

"So what happened to put the deal in the toilet?"

"Another party showed up. They were interested in the

same artifacts as the Devil Man. One artifact in particular and they even knew where to find it. All they needed was our help with retrieval. The woman offered me ten million for a one-time job. Seemed like a good deal, so I said yes. The mission was a success, though a number of explorers died."

"Interesting definition of success," Jinx said.

The brothers all glared at her, but she just crossed her arms and glared back. Daisuke knew how she felt, but at the end of the day no one put a gun to the explorers' heads. They chose a dangerous lifestyle and it cost them.

"Who was this new party?" Daisuke asked.

Emile looked back at him. It seemed the brothers were content to let him handle the discussion. "I don't know who she worked for. All she said was that her name was Vanessa and that she'd pay me ten million if we helped retrieve the artifact."

"Let me guess. Tall, figure to die for, dark hair with a white streak over the left eye."

Emile's eyes widened. "Do you know her?"

"Not well. Vanessa Warhawk works for an organization opposed to mine. They may well be worse than the Cult of Abaddon."

"That would be an impressive feat," Emile said. "Anyway, the team returned and I went to meet her so I could deliver the artifact. I barely arrived when a demon showed up and attacked us. Vanessa fought it and I ran for my life. I warned my brothers, but Timothy was too slow. Cultists grabbed him. The deal was that we would meet in Paris should anything happen. I keep hoping I'm wrong and he'll show up, but when that assassin appeared, I had to accept that he wasn't going to."

"I'm sorry about your brother. Do you still have the artifact?"

Emile nodded, pulled a seal out of his pocket, and placed it on the table. "Doesn't look like much considering all the death and destruction it's brought into my life. What are you going to do?

Daisuke took his metal card out and summoned his trunk. "I'm going to make sure no one can ever use the seal for evil again. Then I'm going to find the Devil Man and make him return my friend. If your brother is still alive, I'll do my best to free him as well."

Hope and resignation warred on the brothers' faces. Daisuke took out his phone, snapped a picture of the seal and texted it to the boss. He needed the demon's name before he could fuse the seal with the Staff of Law. Shouldn't take her too long to look it up.

Master, the hellfire demon from London is coming this way, quickly.

"Shit!" Daisuke grabbed the staff and put his trunk away.

"What is it?" Jinx asked.

"Our fiery friend from London is on his way. Looks like our missing Blaze brother has been talking."

"Timothy would never betray us!" one of the other brothers said.

"Your faith in your brother is admirable, but you have no idea what someone might do when exposed to the tender mercies of the Cult of Abaddon. On the plus side, hopefully that means he's still alive. Now, you all stay in here. Jinx, keep an eye on them. I'll deal with the demon."

"Wait!" Jinx scrambled to grab his arm. "You can't fight that thing alone. I can help."

He patted her hand. "I appreciate the offer, but I've got a

plan. If it doesn't work, you need to get these three to safety. I'm counting on you."

Jinx didn't let go. "I don't care about them. I care about you."

Daisuke smiled. That was sweet, but this really wasn't the time. "Trust me, it'll be fine."

He pulled her hand away and marched through the door. Merging his vision with Ruq's, he spotted the demon about fifty yards out and charging fast. Hopefully his plan would work.

If it didn't, it wouldn't take long to find out.

CHAPTER NINETEEN

Daisuke strode onto the front porch, the Staff of Law clenched tight in his right first. He really hoped his plan worked since fighting a mid-tier hellfire demon one on one didn't overly appeal to him. He could probably kill it if he had to, but it would leave him totally drained.

He sensed the demon getting closer as he stepped down to the ground and moved away from the house. It couldn't be more than twenty yards out now.

Just as the thought crossed his mind, the demon emerged from a clump of trees at the edge of the yard. It was the same one from London, at least judging from the red skin and curved black horns. It had a mark on its forehand, but he couldn't make out the details. If he was wrong about it being the same seal, this was going to get ugly in a hurry.

The demon took one look at Daisuke and charged.

He recited the spell once in his head then prepared himself for battle.

When the demon had covered half the distance separating them, Daisuke hurled a huge black lightning bolt at it. The spell took the demon dead center in the chest and stopped it in its tracks.

He lunged, staff leading.

The demon hopped aside, evading the blow.

Shit!

Daisuke had hoped his spell would buy enough time, but as usual he was doomed to disappointment. He dove and rolled under a blast of hellfire.

A countering burst of black lightning drove the demon back a step but didn't stun it. He needed time, just a couple seconds would be enough.

The demon charged in, claws swinging.

Daisuke backpedaled, making sure to move further from the house and its occupants.

Channeling ether through the staff, he loosed a telekinetic fist that picked the demon up and hurled it ten feet across the yard. It landed with a thud, rolled to its feet, and rushed right back in. Did the damn thing even feel pain? Ruq complained enough that he was pretty sure demons did, but this one certainly gave no sign of it.

A particularly hard backhanded blow forced Daisuke to block with the staff. Then it was his turn to go flying.

Enhanced physical abilities allowed him to land unharmed and on his feet. Unharmed or not, he wouldn't want to take many more hits like that.

He was debating his next move when shadow webs appeared and wrapped up the demon. It thrashed and howled as it struggled to free itself.

Daisuke didn't waste his chance.

He darted in and drove the staff into the seal on the

monster's head. "By the blood of Solomon that flows through my veins I command you to merge."

The spell activated and a vibration ran through the staff. When he stepped back he found a new seal in place. That took care of phase one. The demon continued to thrash around, finally ripping the shadow webs apart. It seemed stealing the seal did nothing to weaken it.

He took a breath to shout a command when something weird happened. The demon's face ripped in half, one side red and demonic and the other human and twisted in pain. The sickening sound of ripping flesh continued as demon and human separated until two distinct figures remained.

The human cultist fell to the ground, unconscious.

The demon raised a clawed hand to pierce his back.

"Dostrik, stop!" Daisuke shouted.

The demon froze mid blow. It glared at Daisuke with burning red eyes. Ordinarily he'd have no qualms about letting the demon send his former partner to Abaddon's hell, but today Daisuke needed answers and he wasn't sure which of the two was most likely to have them.

"Daisuke!" Jinx came sprinting over and wrapped her arms around him. "I thought that thing was going to kill you."

"He was certainly giving it his best shot." Much as he enjoyed Jinx's hug, this was no time for such things. "Can you web up the cultist and bring him back to the house? I need to ask him some questions. I'll be right behind you."

Jinx obliged him and when she'd gotten on her way he focused all his will on the demon. "Dostrik, in the name of Solomon and by my blood and the power of the staff you are bound. You will stay here. You will not move until I command you otherwise."

Daisuke felt the spell settle around Dostrik. He also felt every drop of evil and hate the demon could send his way. It was a fair bit, but nothing compared to Vorgon. Content that his prisoner wouldn't be going anywhere for the foreseeable future, he hurried to catch up with Jinx.

He reached her in the doorway to the dining room. Jinx stood with her hand to her mouth staring at three dead bodies. The brothers had been slain, their throats cut so deeply that it was a wonder their heads were still attached. They had also been stabbed through the heart for good measure. Of the mystery seal, there was no sign.

Ruq, what happened?

I saw no one enter or leave, Master. Whoever did this must have been a wizard and a skilled one at that.

Daisuke cursed the universe. Genuinely talented wizards seldom joined demon cults. They had no need to sell their souls to demons to gain power. This had to be the one mentioned in the journal.

Maybe it was a priest using Abaddon's power in a creative way.

I would've sensed it. I did come from Abaddon's hell after all.

"Shit!"

"It's my fault," Jinx said. "You told me to watch over them and I disobeyed. They died because of my failure. I'm so sorry."

"Done is done. There's nothing we can do for them now."

Daisuke's phone chose that moment to ping with an incoming message. It was the demon's name and rank. Razak, elder demon in the service of Abaddon. Great, a hell-fire demon as powerful as Vorgon and they let his seal slip right through their fingers. This mission wasn't going at all according to plan.

"What do we do now?" Jinx asked in a timid voice.

He kicked the cultist over on his back a little bit harder than strictly necessary. "Now we hope this piece of shit can tell us something useful. I'd very much like to get ahold of that seal before someone uses it to free Razak."

It was really hard to tell how much time had passed since Helena arrived. Sitting in the dim dungeon with a silent Vanessa for company did nothing to make the time go by more quickly. Much as she disliked the woman, Helena figured they were going to have to work together if they wanted to get out of their current predicament alive.

She shifted, but the hard stone floor didn't really have any comfortable spots. There wasn't so much as a cot to sleep on or a pot to piss in. What passed for a bathroom was a hole in the far corner of the cell. A quick look earlier confirmed that there was no hope of escape that way. At least not without access to her magic.

Across the way, Timothy Blaze hadn't uttered a sound or moved an inch since she arrived. Only the very faint rise and fall of his chest let her know that he was still alive. She doubted that would last for much longer.

Unable to stand the silence, Helena turned to Vanessa. "Do you know how many cultists there are?"

Vanessa turned her indifferent gaze toward Helena. "I haven't the least idea. Six is the most I've seen, but there could be more wandering around. They also have at least two lesser demons at their command. That's more than enough to deal with us even if we had some way to get out of this cage, which we don't."

"What the hell's wrong with you? I didn't take the members of the Blood of Solomon for fatalists. I pictured you as the sort that would fight to the very end."

"Were I capable of fighting, I would happily do so, if only in the hope that I might take a cultist or two down with me." Vanessa said that last bit with enough venom to make Helena hope that she had at least a little bit of spirit left.

"There was one upstairs. He was hiding behind a man I took to be the Devil Man, at least judging by how the others deferred to him. There's something about the way he held himself. As if he had a secret."

"Remi Velung. Couldn't be anyone else. If I could only kill one cultist, he'd be my choice."

"Friend of yours?"

Vanessa snorted at that. "He was. Remi is of the blood. For three years he served Lord Solomon loyally as a researcher and archivist in our library. Little did we know he was only using us to gain knowledge. When he saw a better opportunity, he left. To team up with the Devil Man of all things. He calls himself the Devil's Shadow now. His betrayal stings even worse than Daisuke's refusal to join us in the first place. That decision, wrong as it is, at least has the virtue of being honest."

Helena couldn't feel bad for the Blood of Solomon, but her concern about their situation did rise several notches. Those with the blood were among the strongest wizards in the world. That one of them was here and allied with the high priest of Abaddon made the situation so much worse.

"Why would Remi leave one master only to serve someone else? I would think he'd be more apt to strike out on his own."

"How should I know what the lunatic is thinking? My

only interest is in getting out of here, regaining my magic, and ripping his guts out through his ass."

Helena winced at the visual. "Charming."

There was a clunk from the entrance and a moment later Yorn came stomping into view. He held two plates of food and two cups of water. He set them on the floor and slid them through the slot in the door.

"How long are you planning on keeping us here?" Helena demanded.

"Until the time of your sacrifice," Yorn said. "Are you so eager to meet your end on Abaddon's altar?"

Helena was surprised he answered. Eager for more information she responded, "I'm eager to get out of this cell. The boredom may well kill me before your master can sacrifice me."

"You're in luck. One of our agents has succeeded in claiming the final artifact and killing the traitors. Once this one expires—" Yorn turned to spit on Timothy "—they will all be dead."

Helena's throat tightened. Daisuke was after the Blaze brothers as well. If they were dead then something might have happened to him.

No! She couldn't think like that.

He wouldn't be taken out so easily. Especially with Jinx backing him up, much as she hated to admit it.

"Soon our master will ascend to immortality and this world will kneel at his feet." With that grandiose statement, Yorn turned and marched back the way he'd come.

"Well, shit!" Vanessa said. "The cult already had the prison, if they've got the seal now as well, things could get really out of hand in a hurry."

"Do you know which demon it is?" Helena got up and

collected her food. After a moment's hesitation she grabbed Vanessa's as well and brought it to her. The greasy stew was by no means appetizing, but she was determined to keep her strength up.

"We don't know its name, but Lord Solomon was pretty confident that it was Abaddon's elder demon."

Helena sat back down. Of course it was the most powerful one Abaddon sent. It wasn't like anyone would go to all this trouble for an imp.

She ate a mouthful of stew, grimaced as she choked down some gristle, and asked, "Do you know why they're so interested in sacrifices, I mean besides the obvious? You can open a demon's prison and command the demon without needing to kill someone first."

Vanessa shook her head. "No clue, though you can be sure Remi has something to do with it. The use of life force to empower magic was one of his areas of interest according to the assistant archivist. I'm afraid we're going to find out the hard way."

Helena feared that too. And locked in this cage, there wasn't a thing she could do about it.

CHAPTER TWENTY

Daisuke slapped the unconscious cultist hard across the face. There was no time to screw around being polite. Every second the seal got further away. Daisuke had a pretty good idea where it was going, but he didn't want to run into Castle Ravenclaw blind. He'd tried that before and nearly got himself killed for his trouble.

The cultist groaned and opened his eyes. When he saw Daisuke looming over him he flinched.

"You'd better flinch, you son of a bitch. I'm going to ask you some questions. If you don't answer them to my satisfaction, I'll feed you to your pet demon. Let's start with your name and the name of whoever killed the Blaze boys."

"A demon loyal to Abaddon would never harm a fellow servant. Save your meaningless threats for someone that fears them."

"For a demon cultist you're remarkably ignorant when it comes to demonic behavior. Demons obey those with the power to compel them. They don't give a damn about mortals, even those who worship their master. If I tell

Dostrik to devour you starting from your feet and working his way up, he'll do it without batting an eye. Would you like me to have him gnaw your left arm off as a demonstration?"

"You can't scare me. Even if I die, I'll be reborn in Abaddon's hell. There I will be rewarded for my loyal service."

Daisuke hated true believers.

"Fine, have it your way. I'll just rip the information I need straight out of your brain. I hope you enjoy life as a drooling vegetable." That last bit was mostly a final threat to hopefully get him to talk. Alas the cultist just clamped his jaw shut and glared in stony silence.

Daisuke knelt and touched the cultist's forehead. Much like with the nearly dead priest of the Binder, mind reading was far from an exact science, but hopefully he could get enough information to figure out what was actually going on.

Ether flowed out, connecting Daisuke to the cultist's brain. Dark images appeared one after another. People died as this asshole cut out their hearts and tossed them into a raging pillar of hellfire. He looked closer. They weren't memories, they were fantasies.

Snarling away his annoyance, Daisuke shattered the disgusting thoughts and moved deeper. The closest ones were tinged with red and showed the cultist approaching from within the demon's body. He went back far enough to watch the cultist don the mask that held Dostrik's seal. The transformation was invisible, but the memory of the pain involved remained crystal clear.

Interesting that through the entire string of memories there was nothing about whoever killed the Blaze brothers. It seemed unlikely, but maybe the assassin was working for another group.

He skimmed through some memories of the slaughter in London before reaching something from Castle Ravenclaw. Nicholas—he finally found someone using the cultist's name —was speaking with a hooded individual that he held in high esteem and no small amount of fear. He rewound to the very beginning of the conversation and let it play.

The man's hood went back. Sure enough, it was the high priest of Abaddon. Daisuke didn't know his real name, but he had to be the one calling himself the Devil Man. The conversation primarily concerned Nicholas receiving his demon mask, what they called the artifact.

When the Devil Man finished up, a second dark figure appeared. The high regard vanished and the fear spiked. Whoever the new guy was, Nicholas was more afraid of him than the Devil Man. The newcomer gave a warning about not wearing the mask for too long lest his mind fully merge with the demon. If that happened, he'd no longer be able to return to his human form.

The memory ended and Daisuke went looking for more information about Castle Ravenclaw. He saw empty corridors, a passage down to the dungeon which came with an overwhelming desire not to go down the steps lest he lose his ability to cast spells for a day. That was good to know. If Helena was there, without her magic, she'd have no hope of escaping.

Looked like there were no more than half a dozen actual cultists, but he did see several demons like the one he killed in Venice. That matched what Jinx read in the journal. None of them would be a huge deal for him, but plenty of trouble for any non-wizards that had the misfortune to visit the castle.

He searched for a few more minutes, but that was pretty

much everything of any interest. It was with great relief that he left Nicholas's twisted mind.

Daisuke stood and stretched. He'd stiffened up during the process. Not at all an uncommon occurrence and it was worse the nastier the memories he looked at.

"Are you okay?" Jinx asked.

"Yeah, no problem. I'm pretty sure Helena is in Castle Ravenclaw like we thought." He gave her the gist of what he found out. "I need to update the boss, then we're headed for Romania. If we're lucky we can get there before the assassin. Not that I'm overly optimistic."

"What about the demon? Are you just going to leave it in the yard? That seems dangerous."

"No, I'll have it move out of sight in the barn. Until we retrieve Dostrik's prison, there's nothing else I can do." Daisuke dug out his phone and dialed. "Boss, I've got bad news and worse news. Which do you want first?"

"Just give me all of it."

She sounded more on edge than usual. That couldn't be good. "Okay, here goes. The Blaze brothers are dead and the assassin, who appears to be a wizard and not a priest, has Razak's seal. I'm also pretty sure the Devil Man is Abaddon's high priest and that he's got Helena locked up in Castle Ravenclaw's dungeon."

"That's all terrible news. As for me, Donny finished his analysis of the ring. Turns out there's a wizardly skin over a core of demon magic."

"That jives with what I've learned. Looks like there're at least a couple wizards working with the cult. Why in heaven's name they'd want to work with the mad fools is another matter."

"People do all sorts of crazy things. You're going to the castle?"

"Not much choice if we want to save Helena and prevent Razak's summoning and I very much want to do both. I also want to kill the Devil Man and his flunkies. That he escaped the first time is one of the bigger disappointments in my life. I'm also going to have to leave Dostrik here. Unless you have a better idea."

"You could destroy him."

Daisuke grimaced. "I could, but it would take a lot out of me and we don't have time for a full recovery. This mission is going to be tough enough without me being at less than full strength."

"In that case, do what you think best. There's a barrier around the castle, so I recommend you appear somewhere nearby."

"Good plan. I'll call when I have news."

"Best of luck, Daisuke." The boss hung up and he pocketed his phone.

It was time to get going, but first... He pointed at Nicholas and a thread of ether wrapped around the man's heart. A burst of lightning blew it to pulp. One less cultist in the world could only be a good thing. Hopefully he could rid the world of a few more today.

CHAPTER TWENTY-ONE

A few seconds after depositing Dostrik in the barn at the Blazes' farm, Daisuke and Jinx emerged from a shadow at the edge of the town of Tamaz about six miles from Castle Ravenclaw. It was the same town he'd used as his base the first time he explored the castle, so he knew it well. The town, or village to be more accurate, consisted of a bunch of single-story houses, a general store, and a church of the Goddess, Lady of Healing. And that was it. The locals worked as loggers and farmers for the most part.

"Never thought we'd set foot in this dump again," Ruq said.

"It's like a cooler, slightly better constructed Milden Station," Jinx added.

Neither of them was wrong either. Daisuke frowned and stretched out with the ether. He didn't sense a single life force. Even if most of the locals were at work, there should be some kids and their mothers, the clerks at the store, something. The town felt deader than dead.

"Can't say I like the feel of this."

"Should we check it out?" Jinx asked.

"No time. The road to the castle runs right through the town. We'll see what we can see, but we can't linger."

"At least there's no corruption," Ruq said. "Everyone probably hit the road when the cultists showed up. I can't imagine why they'd want to live in the shadow of that creepy castle anyway."

"I imagine it was more of a necessity than a choice. The original cult didn't seem to bother them after all." Daisuke set out from the edge of the woods toward the town proper.

It didn't get any better looking as they closed in. The silence was eerie. It felt like walking through a graveyard. His gaze darted left and right, alert for any danger. Not that any presented itself.

"Check a couple houses," Daisuke said.

Ruq flew to the nearest building and looked in the window. "No bodies on the floor and no sign that anyone was forced to leave against their will."

He checked a few more and found the exact same amount of nothing. And then they were through and on to climbing a gentle slope that led to the castle. The dirt road showed signs of use, but not very recent. Probably gangsters coming to buy demons. There was a thought Daisuke didn't want to dwell on for too long.

They'd covered about three miles when Jinx asked, "Shouldn't there be patrols or something?"

"Everything I've seen leads me to believe there aren't that many cultists or demons. They're probably focusing their efforts on protecting the castle itself. That said, we should be getting close to the barrier the boss mentioned. Depending on how it's set up, that might send out an alarm."

Something dark passed over them but by the time Daisuke looked up he only caught a glimpse of whatever it was. He really wanted to think bird, but that seemed incredibly naive especially given the complete lack of wildlife in the area. More likely it was some nasty thing that would be trying to kill them shortly.

"What happens if an alarm goes off?" Jinx asked.

"Then we deal with whatever comes after us."

Daisuke trudged on for another mile or so then a faint tingle ran through him. That had to signal the edge of the barrier. Ahead of them, Castle Ravenclaw loomed large. There was no movement on the battlements, but the portcullis was closed, so clearly the cult wasn't expecting guests.

A blood-curdling howl went up and a moment later a demon leapt over the wall. It was vaguely humanoid, but ran on all fours like a beast. Its hairless, fish-belly-white skin gleamed with some sort of slime. It wasn't the ugliest demon he'd ever seen, but it was close.

"Ew," Jinx said.

That pretty well summed up Daisuke's feelings.

The demon made no effort at stealth. It just charged at them full speed. Twenty yards out it leapt.

As soon as it left the ground, Daisuke pointed and loosed a bolt of black lightning. The spell blasted the demon out of the air. It landed, still twitching, a few feet away. A second blast reduced it to a puddle of gray slime.

"Pathetic," Ruq said.

"I expected to run into something stronger," Jinx agreed.

Daisuke had serious doubts that the minor demon was the worst thing they were going to run into. "There's no way they don't know we're here. No sense holding back on the magic now."

He held out his hand and Jinx took it. A flying spell carried them up and over the castle wall. They landed in the courtyard just as a nervous-looking man emerged from the main keep. He carried a wooden mask in his hand.

Before Daisuke could cast, the cultist said, "Mask, on."

The mask fused with his skin in a process that combined melting and twisting. It was pretty disgusting.

A bolt of black lightning was turned aside by some sort of corrupt barrier. It seemed the castle's real defender had finally arrived.

The cultist had fully transformed into a smaller version of Dostrik: red skin, black horns, and glowing red eyes. That seemed to be the standard hellfire demon look. Its aura of corruption wasn't as strong as Dostrik's, but it was nothing to sneeze at either.

Daisuke waited for the demon to attack, but it seemed content to block the door. Clearly it was more intelligent than the first one Daisuke killed. Its mission had to be stopping them from entering the keep.

"I can beat this thing," Jinx said. "You go help Helena and stop them from freeing Razak."

Daisuke looked from Jinx to the demon and back. That sounded like a terrible idea. Instead he took out his phone and snapped a picture of the demon's face. If he could find out the demon's name, he could take control of it the same way he did Dostrik.

Unfortunately, when he got ready to send the text, he had no signal.

"So much for that plan."

"I can do this," Jinx said. "Trust me."

A vibration ran through the ether making it clear he didn't have much choice. "All right, but don't you dare get yourself killed. I'll start the ball rolling then he's all yours."

Daisuke pointed and a black disk formed under the demon. It leapt aside, but the pillar of black lightning still grazed it. Having done all he could, Daisuke ran for the door.

Daisuke didn't look back as he ran through the open keep door and into the castle proper. He had to trust Jinx to handle the demon. He knew how strong she was. That would have to be enough.

It felt like déjà vu when he entered the plain gray stone walls. It hadn't been so many years ago that he first visited the castle and now here he was, back again. Not a situation he remotely expected to find himself in.

"Get to the dungeon and free Helena."

"Sure you won't need me to back you up?" Ruq asked.

Daisuke's lip quirked up at that. "I'm willing to risk it. Free her and get to safety. Without her magic, Helena won't be of any help in the fight."

"You think it'll be that easy to convince her?"

"Stubborn as she can be at times, Helena has to know that the best way she can help is to get out of the line of fire. Once she's safe it will be one less thing I have to worry about."

"Fine, good luck." Daisuke sensed Ruq fly off toward the dungeon entrance. No one knew the castle better than his familiar, so he should have no trouble getting Helena out and to safety.

Putting the matter firmly out of his mind, Daisuke made a sharp right-hand turn down the hall that led to the main altar chamber. If they were going to summon Razak, that's where it would happen.

Remi sensed his agent approaching a moment before she knocked on his workshop door. He stood, walked over, and opened it. Outside, his lovely servant, Vixen, waited. Redhaired and dressed in a simple black top and skirt, she was a unique creature he made in his lab back at the Blood of Solomon's base. A fusion of human and fire spirit, she was his first successful test of the magical principles that undergirded the demon masks. Best of all, her loyalty was above reproach.

She bowed and held Razak's seal out to him. "Success, Master."

He took the seal and smiled. "I didn't doubt you for a moment, my dear. Well done. Now we can finally move on to the final phase of the plan."

"What do you wish me to do, Master?" Vixen asked in her dull, monotone voice.

"For now just stay close and remain invisible. Should things not go exactly as I intend, it will be good to have you to hand."

"As you command." She took a step back and vanished.

Remi shifted his gaze to the ether and could see her outline, but no one without magic would have any idea she was present. It would've been nice to have some way of hiding her from the Devil Man, but the high priest already knew Vixen existed so it was kind of pointless.

He closed his workshop door and strode down to the Devil Man's chamber. Two quick knocks brought him to the door. Without a word Remi held up the seal.

The Devil Man took it, caressing it like it was his long-lost lover. "At last. At last we can free Razak and I can become a god."

That was such an exaggeration Remi wouldn't have known what to say had he cared to comment. "You should send Yorn for the prisoners. The sooner we free Razak the better."

"Quite right. We will welcome the elder demon with a proper sacrifice. It's only fitting to offer a gift before we become one."

Remi fell in behind the Devil Man as they made their way through the empty halls toward the altar chamber. It was hard to imagine this place once housing scores of cultists. That had been long before Remi's time with the group, still, he imagined it was quite a sight. After all, it was rare to see more than a dozen fools in one place.

When they reached the altar chamber, Yorn and Velcan were both waiting. The Devil Man must've summoned them without Remi noticing the magic. That was an impressive feat all on its own.

Before anyone had a chance to speak, a tremor ran through the ether. Someone had just triggered the ward around the castle. He'd been expecting uninvited guests to show up, but they were going to be too late.

"Did you feel it?" Remi asked.

"Indeed. We have some unwelcome company about to arrive at a most inopportune time. Yorn, fetch the sacrifices. Velcan, man the door. If the minor claw demon can't slay the intruders, it will fall to you to either kill them or at least delay them long enough that they don't interrupt the ceremony."

Both cultists bowed and said, "Yes, Master," in perfect unison.

Orders given, the Devil Man walked over to the altar where Razak's prison rested. He ran the seal around the edge of the bronze cylinder, drawing a wince from Remi. He couldn't free the demon until the sacrifices arrived. If he did, all of Remi's plans would fall apart.

"What will you do when I rule the world?" the Devil Man asked. "The few rewards you requested seem insufficient for all that you've done to aid the cause. In truth, without your help, I doubt we would've gotten anywhere close to ultimate victory."

"Having the freedom and resources to pursue my research is all I ever wanted. My former leader always had other things he wanted me to work on and I barely had any time for my own interests. It was most frustrating."

"I can well imagine. Well, rest assured, soon you will have all you could ever want and more."

Remi lowered his head to hide his smile. Indeed, the fool had no idea how right he was.

Helena heard footsteps approaching and got a sick feeling in her stomach. They'd eaten less than two hours ago and bringing them food was the only reason their captor ever came down here. If he was coming back now, it could only mean trouble.

She hopped to her feet and pressed her back against the wall. Whatever happened, she meant to go down fighting.

"Hey," Helena said. "Someone's coming."

"I'm not deaf." Vanessa pushed herself to her feet. "And you know who's coming as well as I do. Only one of them ever comes down here."

"It's two against one and I'm not stiff and sore from being tied up in the trunk of a car. I think we can take him."

"I didn't take you for a complete moron, but maybe I was overly generous." Vanessa heaved a sigh. "Still, better to fight to the bitter end."

Of all the people Helena wouldn't have wanted at her back in a fight, Vanessa had to be near the top of the list. But then again, how did the saying about beggars and choosers go? If it got her out of this dungeon alive, she'd fight with the Reaper himself.

Yorn appeared, two sets of manacles in his hands, and looked from one woman to the other. "Are you going to make this difficult for me? The master is in a hurry. If you resist, I won't be gentle."

"Considering what you have planned for us," Helena said. "I see no reason to go easy on you."

"Have it your way." Yorn unlocked the door and took a step through.

As soon as he did, Helena charged and kicked the door with all her strength in the hope that she might drive it into his leg.

It didn't so much as budge in his grasp.

She narrowly avoided a backhand that no doubt would have put her out of commission. How could he be that strong?

"That was impressive," Vanessa said.

"I don't see you doing anything to help."

Yorn stepped the rest of the way into the cell, and closed and locked the door behind him. The key went in his pocket and the manacles ended up clattering to the floor.

Helena went left and Vanessa right. Whichever of them Yorn went after, the other could attack him from behind.

Yorn's dark, beady eye narrowed even further as he glared at them. He seemed uncertain what to do and Helena was content to wait for him to make the first move. Every second they delayed was a second longer they weren't on their way to the altar.

With a little growl, Yorn lunged at Helena.

She dodged out of the way and kicked him in the knee. It was like striking a tree trunk only harder.

Vanessa darted in and punched him in the ribs to equally little effect.

"I'm going to enjoy watching the master cut your hearts out."

Yorn charged at Helena, arms spread, giving her no good options to dodge.

She leapt straight up.

Yorn wrapped his arms around her ankles and pulled her down to the floor. The impact drove the air out of her lungs. Out of the corner of her eye she saw Vanessa run for the door. Somehow she'd pickpocketed the key.

The door squeaked open and she sprinted away.

Helena was on her own.

CHAPTER TWENTY-TWO

When Daisuke arrived, the altar chamber door was wide open. Not trusting that for a second, he scanned the entry for traps or any other dangerous magic. To his considerable surprise, the doorway was clear.

Beyond it waited an intimidating stone chamber filled with benches lined up facing a gray stone altar covered with a bloodred cloth depicting Abaddon's hellfire symbol. Razak's prison rested in the exact center of the altar. Behind it stood two men in black robes. He recognized both from Nicholas's memories. The larger of the two was the Devil Man and the smaller the Devil's Shadow. A little ways to the right he could make out the indistinct outline of an invisible figure. Impossible to say who or what it was, though the outline was vaguely feminine in shape.

Readying his defenses and taking a tighter grip on the Staff of Law, Daisuke strode into the room.

"You either have great courage or no brains to walk in here alone," the Devil Man said.

"Plenty of dead men have thought the same. When you get to hell, you can exchange notes."

The Devil Man threw back his head and laughed. When his head snapped forward, a gout of hellfire shot out of his mouth straight at Daisuke.

He dove and rolled under the blast before countering with black lightning. His target wasn't the men, but the altar, or more precisely the prison. It went flying along with chunks of shattered stone.

"No!" the Devil's Shadow shouted. "He can't be allowed to interfere. Forget the sacrifices. We'll summon Razak now and bind him to you later. Vixen, keep him busy!"

Daisuke had an instant to wonder who Vixen was before the invisible figure launched itself toward him. He slammed the staff on the floor, sending a rolling wave of force outwards. It slammed into Vixen and sent her tumbling backwards. In the process it dispelled her invisibility, revealing an attractive woman that had obviously been magically altered in some way.

Before she could recover, he sent another blast of normal lightning at the prison, sending it flying further away from the cultists. Daisuke sprinted after them, his attention divided between both groups of enemies.

Another blast of hellfire came roaring his way.

An ethereal wall appeared and angled the blast away from him and toward Vixen, driving the now-recovered woman back.

Daisuke grinned. It was always good to use the enemy's own power against him.

The Devil Man reached the prison first. He had the seal in his right hand and started to bring it into place.

Daisuke spun the staff in a circle, summoning a mini

tornado which he hurled at the Devil Man. The second cultist got in the way and raised both hands. Ether gathered around them as he tried to stop the spell.

He partially succeeded. Most of the energy was dissipated, but enough got through to send the Devil's Shadow flying backwards into his master. Both men went sprawling across the floor. The prison went one way and the seal the other.

Daisuke ignored everyone else and went for the seal.

"Vixen! Get the seal and meet us in my lab!" the Devil's Shadow said.

With unbelievable speed, Vixen shot past Daisuke and snatched up the seal. She had to slow to get it and when she did, a stone spear shot up and pierced her left leg through the calf, nearly ripping the muscle off the bone.

Vixen never made a sound and half limped half ran toward a door in the rear of the chapel.

A bolt of black lightning crashed into the wall just behind her and then she was gone. He snarled and turned to deal with the other two only to see them vanish down a hidden slide behind the altar, taking the prison along with them.

He wanted to scream but lacked the time. Vixen was leaving a blood trail a blind man could follow. The sooner he caught up with her and acquired the seal, the better.

Ruq flew, invisible, down the castle hall. He hated this place. Nothing but bad memories. The worst one being that he ended his career with the cult locked in a cage and left to die. Only slightly less bad than that was the fact that none of the cultists ever gave him sweets. His current master was much more reasonable in that regard. Ruq hoped he didn't get himself killed. That would sever his link to this world and send him directly back to Abaddon's hell.

Given that he was currently betraying the lord of that hell directly, his welcome would no doubt be painful. All the more reason to rescue his master's demon-hating female as quickly as possible. Once that was done, he could hurry back and help sting the Devil Man to death.

He rounded a corner and nearly flew into the chest of an approaching cultist. The ambient corruption had stopped him from sensing the approaching life force. Slung over his shoulder was the unconscious figure of Helena. Search ended, Ruq swung around and swooped in, tail leading. His stinger slammed into the human's neck.

And bounced off.

A backhanded swat sent Ruq tumbling through the air. It didn't actually hurt him, but it did come as a surprise. Could the human see him? From the way he was staring around like an idiot, Ruq thought not. The problem was, if the imp couldn't sting him to death, he had limited other options. He was only two feet tall and not particularly strong after all.

Why was nothing ever easy?

He caught himself before he hit the wall and flew up near the ceiling. Maybe he could get his stinger into the man's eye. Those were usually soft and squishy.

"Show yourself, coward!" the human bellowed. "My master awaits this sacrifice. I will not be delayed."

Ruq chuckled to himself. With any luck, *his* master had already killed the Devil Man. Alright, let's give it another try.

This time he glided down, silent as an owl at midnight, and thrust his stinger right at the human's left eye.

And missed.

He turned his head at the last moment and Ruq's stinger bounced off his temple without so much as scratching the skin. How was a human with no visible magic resisting his attacks?

Ruq snapped his wings, avoiding the human's right hand by inches. Safely hovering just below the ceiling, Ruq debated how best to kill him.

For his part, the man dropped Helena and glared around. "Show yourself! If we're going to fight, let's fight. My master's task must not be delayed."

Did this fool think Ruq would become visible and fight fair just because he yelled some commands? Humans were remarkably strange creatures.

Through their link, Ruq sensed his master's battle raging. Thankfully there was no pain, which meant he hadn't been wounded. That was always a good sign. Sometimes his master got careless and something bad would happen. It seemed he was on his game today.

On the floor, Helena let out a little groan and shifted. Maybe if they worked together Ruq could get in a kill shot. But how to contact her? He had no mystical connection with Helena, which meant no telepathy and Ruq certainly wasn't going to fly down there and whisper in her ear. This odd human, unlikely as it seemed, might have some way to hurt Ruq and there were few things he liked less than being hurt.

"If you walk away and leave the woman," Ruq said. "There's no need for us to fight. Killing you isn't my objective."

And that was the truth, though killing him would certainly be a nice bonus.

"Her life belongs to Abaddon. Her sacrifice will bring my master the power he's destined to wield."

Ruq shook his head. He'd seen late-night movies with better dialogue.

On the floor, Helena shifted so her legs were directly behind the cultist. That might work.

"Now die, human fool!" Ruq flashed into visibility and dove at the man.

He darted left and right, shimmering in and out of view in the hope that he'd confuse the idiot.

It worked. He took a step back and stumbled over Helena's shins. The cultist staggered and tumbled over backwards.

Invisible again, Ruq beat his wings for all he was worth.

When the cultist hit the ground he shouted, whether in pain or anger Ruq didn't know. All he knew was that an open mouth was a perfect target. A squirt of poison jetted out of his stinger and hit the bullseye. The human reflexively swallowed.

Perfect.

It took only a moment for him to start thrashing and convulsing.

That was unusual. Ruq's poison usually killed far more quickly and quietly than that. At last he went still.

Ruq kept his distance just in case. "Hey. Kick him in the head and make sure he's dead."

"He's not breathing," Helena said. "Where's Daisuke?"

"People can hold their breath. Humor me."

Helena snarled at him, but finally gave the unmoving cultist a kick to the temple. He didn't so much as flinch. That was dead enough for Ruq, who shimmered into view.

"My master is currently trying to keep an elder demon from being summoned. Since we're all still alive, I assume he succeeded."

"Take me to him."

"Can you use your magic?" Ruq asked.

Her eyes narrowed and she frowned. "No."

"Then you'll just be in the way. Let's go see if Jinx has finished off the hellfire demon outside. If she has, you can wait there while she and I go help Daisuke."

Helena looked like she wanted to argue, not that it would do any good. The last thing his master needed right now was a distraction. And a defenseless female that he had feelings for was about the most distracting thing Ruq could think of.

She must have realized it too. "Fine. Lead the way."

Thank the universe for a reasonable female.

Ruq flew toward the exit. Hopefully they'd find a victorious Jinx and not an angry demon waiting for them.

As soon as Daisuke vanished into the castle, Jinx focused all her attention on the demon. His spell had grazed it, but didn't seem to do much damage. A few dark lines ran through its red skin marking where the black lightning struck. Despite how confident she'd tried to sound, Jinx wasn't really sure she could beat this thing.

The demon glared at the open door.

She couldn't let it chase after Daisuke. A mental command sent her summoned shadows in to attack.

A single slash of its talons shredded the shadows to dark wisps.

Okay, so much for that brilliant idea. At least she now had the monster's full attention. It spat hellfire at her and Jinx dodged right.

Her counterblast of negative energy slammed into its

chest, staggering it back a step and leaving a dark spot behind. Her magic wasn't totally ineffective, that was a relief. On the downside, she couldn't tell how much damage the attack did. That blast would've killed an ordinary human.

The demon roared and charged her.

Wanting nothing to do with a close encounter of the clawed kind, she raced for the nearest shadow, leapt into it, and emerged behind the demon. A second lance of dark energy burned into its back, this time drawing a pained howl.

Was the back its weak spot?

It spun to face her and she hit it again, this time in the chest. The demon shrugged it off and sent a counterstream of hellfire at her.

Jinx vanished into the shadow paths again. That spell had pretty much confirmed that it was weak on the back side. She didn't know how many shots it would take to kill the thing, but she was good for about a dozen before she'd be too weak to fight. If that happened, she had no doubt the demon would rip her to shreds.

She emerged behind it and blasted it in the back again. This time her spell drove it to its knees. Before it could rise, she hit it again, driving it all the way to the ground.

"I know you're in there," Jinx said. "Take the mask off and surrender and I promise I won't kill you. Please, let this madness end before anyone dies."

The demon roared and surged forward, evading her hastily hurled spell. It sprinted around the courtyard, far too quickly for her to manage an accurate shot.

Jinx cursed herself for being softhearted. She should've kept the pressure on when she had it down. Now she had to clean up her own mess. At least no one could say she didn't give the man inside the demon a chance to surrender.

She stepped back into the shadows and watched. The demon ran around for a few more seconds then seemed to realize she wasn't there any longer. It slowed and finally stopped, looking all around as if expecting to find her.

Jinx waited until it turned away from her, offered a silent word of apology, and stepped out, ready to blast it again.

The demon must have known that was her plan. As soon as she appeared, it spun and rushed right at her.

She tried to slip back into the shadow, but was a fraction too slow. A razor-sharp claw sliced across her stomach, opening a shallow cut. Jinx clamped her jaw shut against the pain and looked down. Blood stained the front of her clothes, but it didn't seem too bad, just ugly.

Lucky for her, as a half demon, she was sturdier than a human.

Not that she had any desire to get hit again.

In the real world, the demon was crouched and ready, looking in every direction, offering no openings.

Jinx wasn't sure what to do. Another mistake was liable to be her last.

The demon snapped around, staring at the castle.

No. Had Daisuke come back? She couldn't let the demon attack him.

Jinx emerged from the shadows directly behind the demon and hit it with every drop of power she could muster. She kept the flow of energy going until it felt like she'd hollowed herself out. At last she fell to her knees gasping for breath.

"Thanks for the rescue."

She looked up to see Ruq flying toward her. Behind him Helena made her way over to the demon.

Or what used to be the demon. The red flesh had melted away, leaving an unmoving human and a mask behind. By some miracle she'd won.

"Daisuke?" she asked.

"Still alive and hunting for the seal and prison." Ruq landed in her lap and transformed into a rat. "We came this way so as not to distract him."

"We should go help him." She nearly laughed when she said it. Just standing might be more than Jinx could handle right now.

"You're done," Ruq said. "Helena can't use her magic at the moment and I'm just an imp and unlikely to be of any use in the sort of fight he's mixed up in. Better if we all stay out here where he won't have to worry about us."

Jinx lay back and stared at the sky. "Is it always like this? Having to hang back and let someone you care about face danger alone?"

"Yes." Helena had left the dead man behind and come over clutching the demon mask in her hands. "And I hate it every time."

Jinx smiled at that. It seemed they'd found something to agree on.

CHAPTER TWENTY-THREE

aisuke hurried along the blood trail Vixen left as she fled the altar chamber. He didn't run, that would be a good way to stumble into a trap, but he did hurry. At least Jinx and Helena were safe. He'd gotten a telepathic message from Ruq a minute ago assuring him that both ladies were fine. Without that to worry about, he was free to fully focus on the matter at hand, namely getting the demon seal before the Devil Man and his flunky.

He listened hard as he went, but the stone halls were silent save for his footfalls. The blood trail rounded a corner. This would be a perfect place for an ambush.

Pausing, Daisuke extended his sight to take a peek. Sure enough, he found an invisible Vixen standing a few feet down the hall. From her position he guessed she was ready to pounce as soon as he appeared. Her wound had already stopped bleeding, confirming that she couldn't be fully human.

Smiling to himself, Daisuke blinked his sight back to his

body and conjured an illusion. He filled it with negative energy and sent it walking around the corner.

A moment later it exploded.

He rushed around the corner, staff leveled, and found Vixen lying on the floor, seemingly unconscious. He'd put enough negative energy in that trap to kill an elephant. Her lifeforce was dimmed, but still present.

Not wanting to fall for a trap himself, Daisuke leveled the staff and loosed a blast of black lightning.

Vixen contorted her body, avoiding the spell, and scrambled to her feet. The woman, or whatever she was, panted for breath. How she was even on her feet, he couldn't begin to guess.

"Drop the seal and surrender," Daisuke said despite having no hope that she'd comply.

As expected Vixen remained silent, glaring at him through narrow, slightly glowing red eyes. The long dagger in her right hand trembled, betraying her weakness. It was a standoff. As soon as he tried to cast a spell, she'd be on him.

There was one thing he could try. Drawing ether into his eyes, Daisuke activated Crimson Haze.

When he did, Vixen arched her back and screamed. It was the first sound she'd made since the battle began. As he thought, whatever nonhuman essence made up part of her being, it was susceptible to his anti-spirit magic.

Vixen collapsed as he burned her away inch by inch. Daisuke didn't know if she was a willing servant or if the cult had bound her somehow. But either way, she had proven herself to be his enemy and his enemies all met the same fate.

When the last of her life force vanished, Daisuke's eyes were stinging and he felt blood running down his cheeks.

Hopefully he'd have at least a few minutes to recover before round two with the Devil Man.

But first things first. He collected Razak's seal and fused it with the staff. With that done, no one should be able to open the prison or control the elder demon. Mission at least partially accomplished.

He stepped over Vixen's body. When he did, a weak hand grabbed his pant leg.

He stopped and turned back. How could she still be alive? Daisuke took a knee.

"Thank you for freeing me," Vixen said.

"You're welcome, I think. What happened to you?"

"Remi bought me at a slave auction and performed some kind of ritual to fuse me with a magical creature." She seemed to gain strength as she spoke. "He controlled the creature and it used my body as its own. I was only a passenger. For years I watched my body perform the most horrible acts of murder while being powerless to stop it. I've wanted to die for so long, but I was too strong. None of my victims could even scratch me. So I thank you for stopping me."

Her life force was fading fast. Daisuke was no dedicated healer like Carter, but he knew a few tricks. Damned if he was going to let another innocent die because of these sons of bitches. Gently weaving ether through Vixen's body, he strengthened her spirit a little at a time, enhancing its connection to her flesh. He also patched up her leg the best he could.

When he finished, she seemed stable if very weak. Satisfied that he'd done all he could for her, he stood and continued down the hall. He checked each room until he found a door sealed with magic and warded with hellfire. This had to be the room he wanted.

Master, are you okay?

I'm fine, Ruq. I've got the seal. The Devil Man and his buddy escaped and I'm in no shape to go after them right now. I'm looking for the other demon prisons so I can seal Dostrik and his little brother away. Did Jinx actually kill the demon?

Not sure. She killed the hell out of his human host, but the mask with the demon seal is still intact.

Well, I'll deal with it later. Stay with Helena and Jinx. I won't be long.

He felt Ruq's consciousness fade to its usual place in the back of his mind and returned his attention to the warded door. An ethereal construct scrubbed away the sealing runes and the magic dissipated. The ordinary lock proved no match for a hard front kick. Inside was a workshop with tables, shelves, books, and all manner of magical paraphernalia. It all needed to be collected and transported back to base, but two things caught his eye at once: a pair of bronze cylinders.

He grabbed them. The rest he could deal with later.

Daisuke closed the door and put a ward of his own on it. It wouldn't stop a determined wizard, but it would slow them down and let him know someone had shown up looking to cause trouble. For now he'd done all he could.

He went back down the hall, scooped up Vixen, and made his way back to the castle entrance. It was time to go home and get some rest and cookies.

Helena stood over the corpse of Velcan and shook her head. For a demon-worshipping cultist, he hadn't been such a bad guy. It always seemed a shame when someone with the potential to be okay got led down the wrong path. Sometimes, usually late at night when she couldn't sleep, Helena wondered what would've happened if Daisuke had agreed to join the Blood of Solomon instead of the Circle.

She shuddered just thinking about it.

Swallowing her regrets about Velcan's fate, she picked up the mask and walked over to check on Jinx. While she considered the woman a rival when it came to Daisuke's affection, she didn't actually dislike her as a person and she was a teammate now. That counted for a lot.

Ruq had curled up in her lap in rat form. Both of them looked up as she approached.

"You two okay?"

Jinx offered a weak smile. "I've been better, but the bleeding's already stopped. My demon blood ensures that I heal quickly. Though I won't be at full strength for a week or so. What about you?"

"Bumps, bruises, and I still can't touch the ether. I don't know what sort of poison they've got in the dungeon, but it's really effective."

"It's not poison, it's miasma," Ruq said. "The foundation of the castle is built using stone brought from Abaddon's hell. It retains the corrupting effects of its source. It doesn't bother demons or undead. Daisuke could probably withstand it for a couple hours if he had to. But for a normal human wizard, the corrupting effects would keep you from being able to use your magic."

"If that's the case, shouldn't I be fine now that I'm away from it? And how did they block me from casting after the demon knocked me out?"

"You absorbed some of the miasma due to long-term exposure. Getting out in the pure ether will purge it in time.

As for your other question, a little bit of powdered demon stone that had been enhanced with a curse mixed into your food or water would do it."

Helena nearly gagged at the idea that Velcan had fed her stone from Hell. She found herself a good deal less sympathetic to his fate.

"Master!" Ruq leapt off Jinx's stomach and flew toward the castle.

Helena spun, smiled when she saw Daisuke looking more or less intact, and immediately frowned when she noticed the beautiful woman in his arms. Another one. How did he keep finding them?

"Who's that?" Helena asked.

"Her name's Vixen. The cult grafted a spirit into her body and used it to control her. Somehow she survived me burning the spirit out, but she's in rough shape. I need to get her to a healer in a hurry. Speaking of, are you two okay?"

"I still can't use my magic, but otherwise I'm fine. I can't believe I'm going to say this, but mostly that's thanks to Ruq."

"It's good that you no longer deny my greatness," Ruq said from his perch on Daisuke's shoulder.

Helena made a face, but for today at least, she'd let him get away with his comments.

"I got pretty beat up." Jinx forced herself to her feet. "But nothing that won't heal in a few days."

"That's a relief. Let's get out of here. Vixen isn't getting any lighter and I can't shadow walk until we're outside the barrier."

"My powers worked fine during the fight," Jinx said.

Daisuke set out for the gate and Helena fell in beside him. Jinx joined the group opposite her.

"Did you try to move beyond the barrier?" he asked.

"No, just short range."

Daisuke nodded. "I suspect if you tried to pass through the barrier, you'd find the passage blocked."

After a brief pause to rust a hole in the portcullis, they set out down the dirt road.

A hundred yards further on Helena asked, "Did you see Vanessa?"

"Nope. If she got loose, I'll bet dinner at your favorite restaurant that she split as fast as her legs could carry her. Especially if her magic was in the same state as yours. She's probably long gone. And good riddance. I'm pretty well tapped out at the moment. I could fight if I had to, but I'm nowhere near my best."

"What about Timothy?" Jinx asked.

"Shit!" Helena said. "I forgot all about him. Last I knew he was still alive in the dungeon. We can't leave him here."

Daisuke's face twisted. "I'll come back for him as soon as we get Vixen to a healer. I'm not sure how glad he'll be to have survived considering what happened to his brothers, but we can't leave him to die either. He should be fine for an hour or two."

That seemed optimistic to Helena, but she was hardly in a position to argue.

They made the rest of the walk in silence and as soon as they passed through the barrier, Jinx carried her through the shadow paths. A few seconds later they emerged in Zurich behind their headquarters.

Home again. By some miracle Helena had survived getting kidnapped by a demon cult. There had been a time in the dungeon where she'd had her doubts. Through it all only one thought kept her from giving up and that was knowing that Daisuke would be coming for her.

And he did, more or less. And he always would. She understood that, even if he didn't love her the way she did him.

For now, that would have to be enough.

The emergency escape tunnel under Abaddon's altar led to an earthen tunnel that had been reinforced with magic. Remi appreciated having a ready escape path, though the Devil Man said only a coward would use it. He glanced at his quote unquote "master" who was busy brushing dirt off his black robes. With the cult destroyed and his plans in ruins, Remi considered killing the arrogant priest and starting over elsewhere.

He dismissed the plan a moment later. For all his stupidity, the Devil Man was still a reasonably powerful magic user and new pawns could always be found. Now that Vanessa had escaped, it was only a matter of time before Solomon the Great sent someone after him. When the inevitable confrontation came, Remi wouldn't object to having a disposable ally on hand.

"We need to circle back to the castle and meet up with your assassin," the Devil Man said. "As long as we can summon Razak, there's still a chance to turn this debacle around."

Remi generally had great faith in Vixen, but when he recognized who was after her, his optimism that she would survive and escape dimmed. It didn't really surprise him that Daisuke was the one that showed up. One thing he'd noticed was that both the Circle and the Blood of Solomon wouldn't hesitate to send someone to rescue one of their members. He assumed the only reason no one came for Vanessa was that Solomon had no one available to send.

"Her opponent is formidable. Vixen may not be up to defeating him."

"He looked like a boy to me." The Devil Man led the way up the tunnel.

"And yet he got past Velcan and forced the two of us to flee. Not an insignificant accomplishment given our combined power."

The Devil Man grunted without further comment.

They trudged through the tunnel for what seemed like a long time, but was probably less than ten minutes before a shiver ran up his spine. Someone, and he had a pretty good idea who, had just destroyed the spirit he'd bound to Vixen's human body. That could only mean that Daisuke had the seal.

Before he could relay the bad news, a light appeared ahead of them and they soon stepped out into the forest surrounding the castle.

"Vixen's dead," Remi said. "It's time to cut our losses and abandon this site."

"I will not flee my home for a second time!"

"Without the demons' power, I fear we have no hope of victory. We need to rebuild. As long as we survive and retain Razak's prison, there's hope for victory. If we go back and get killed, that's the end of everything we hoped to accomplish."

The Devil Man growled then nodded. "My backup hideout is still secure and properly equipped for demon summoning. A handful of cultists and a final demon are waiting as well. The criminals we dealt with owe us favors. The cult will be reformed and then we shall get our revenge."

Remi swallowed a sigh of relief. "A wise decision. Shall we be off?"

The Devil Man stalked away and Remi fell in behind him. For now he would be content to play the obedient follower, but eventually Razak's power would be his.

CHAPTER TWENTY-FOUR

Daisuke was always glad to get home, but today he was a little gladder than usual. Helena unlocked the back door and held it open so he could carry Vixen through. She wasn't horribly heavy, especially since he was using body strengthening magic, but he would still be happy to put her down.

There had been a moment at the castle when he thought Helena was going to give him shit about bringing home another stray, but she'd remained mostly silent about it. He appreciated that.

He hurried past the boss's office and climbed the stairs to the second floor where the recovery rooms were. There were no injured agents using them at the moment so he went to the nearest one and set Vixen on the bed. He checked her spirit through the ether and found it weak but steady. Steady was good. Considering what was done to her, Daisuke suspected she'd have a long road to full recovery.

"Daisuke." He turned and found the boss standing in the

doorway, her ash-gray suit as smooth and wrinkle free as if it had just come from the dry cleaners.

"Hey. You were my next stop."

"Bringing your enemies back now?"

"Vixen isn't an enemy, she's a victim." He explained what happened to her. "These guys seem to have a knack for fusing spirits with other things. I wasn't even sure that was possible. Did you see the mask Helena brought back?"

"I glanced at it. Nasty thing practically reeks of corruption. Come down to my office. The healer is on her way."

He hesitated, not wanting Vixen to wake up and see a strange face. On the other hand, it didn't look like that would be happening any time soon. With a shrug he followed the boss back downstairs.

Jinx and Helena were waiting in her office and Daisuke took the chair between them. He'd been so focused on everything else this was the first time he'd noticed how badly Jinx had been cut. The lines crossing her abdomen were red and angry. The dried blood did nothing to reassure him either.

"Okay, let's hear it," the boss said.

Helena started then Daisuke took over with Jinx chiming in from time to time. When they finished, he said, "Once I get some food and a couple hours' rest, I'm going back for Timothy as well as Remi's research materials. After that it's just a matter of hunting down the Devil Man and Remi."

"I doubt it'll be so easy," the boss said. "You didn't have much luck finding the Devil Man last time he escaped."

"Last time he didn't have Razak's prison. I have the seal and as long as I have that, I can find the prison wherever they might hide it. I suppose they might abandon it, but I'm willing to trade the Devil Man's escape for the prison's recovery."

"Agreed," the boss said. "He's nothing compared to the threat of an elder demon. Okay, we'll go with your plan. Jinx, you nearly died, so you're on rest and recovery for at least two weeks. Helena, you're on recovery until your magic is back to full strength."

"I'm a half demon," Jinx said. "I'll be fine in a few days."

The boss shook her head. "I already cut your recovery time in half to take your unique situation into account. Two weeks, no arguing."

Jinx sighed and Helena grinned. No doubt she had visions of teaming up with him while Jinx was in recovery dancing in her head. Since he was going to be traveling via the shadow paths, that might be tricky. And the truth was, Daisuke could use a day or two of rest time himself. Hopefully once all the loose ends were tied up, he'd get it.

At least until the next emergency sprang up.

Three hours after leaving Castle Ravenclaw, Daisuke was back. Ruq rested on his shoulder as he strode across the empty courtyard toward the keep. A five-thousand calorie meal and a two-hour nap had done wonders to restore his strength. Should a fight be necessary, Daisuke was ready. There should be one more demon and a handful of cultists around here somewhere. With his luck they'd probably fled to cause him trouble in the future.

That was actually okay with him. As soon as he retrieved Timothy, he had two demons to imprison and that always took a toll.

"Considering all the trouble this human and his brothers caused, you should just let him rot," Ruq said.

"Scummy as he might be, leaving the guy in the dungeon of a demon-corrupted castle is a bit much. Of course, considering what Helena said about his condition, I wouldn't be shocked if all we find is a corpse. Since his brothers are dead, that might be a kindness. Whatever the case, it's not my call. I just need to grab him and get the hell out of here. Tearing this vile place down to the foundation and purifying it would make a fine way to spend a month or so, not that I expect to have that kind of free time in the near future."

The keep door was wide open just as he left it. To be on the safe side, he checked for traps and found nothing. He also sensed no demons, or humans for that matter, which confirmed his guess that the rest of the cult had fled along with their master. The miasma in the basement would keep him from sensing Timothy, but the rest of the castle appeared empty as well. Once again it seemed the Devil Man had slipped through his fingers. In a couple of days, he'd get busy rectifying that situation.

Inside they made a quick stop to clean out Remi's lab. Even after emptying his trunk, the material barely fit. With that done, Ruq took point and guided him right to the stairs that led to the dungeon. Daisuke wrapped himself in an anti-corruption barrier. Combined with his natural resistance, that should be plenty for the few minutes he'd be down there. A ball of conjured light went down first and Daisuke followed.

At the bottom of the steps, the miasma washed over him but was turned aside by his barrier. If Helena had to spend days down here, it was no wonder her magic wasn't working.

A quick search confirmed a single occupied cell. Daisuke blasted the lock and stepped inside. Timothy Blaze was, by some miracle, still breathing. His body was covered in burns and bruises. From their angle, it looked like all his fingers had been broken. A crude but effective form of torture.

Right, he could do a full assessment outside. Daisuke conjured a disk under Timothy and quickly retraced his steps to the courtyard. Fresh air had never smelled so sweet.

He paused and sent a stream of ether into Timothy's body. His life force was weak, but the internal damage was minimal. The vital organs were all intact. He was dehydrated and malnourished, but nothing an IV wouldn't fix in a few days.

Timothy groaned and opened his eyes. "Who are you? Where am I?"

"My name is Daisuke and you're in the courtyard of Castle Ravenclaw. I'll be taking you to a hospital presently. You should try and rest."

"My brothers?"

Daisuke hesitated, but it wasn't like there was ever going to be a good time to tell him. "Dead, killed by the cult. You have my condolences."

"I killed them. I was too weak to resist the pain any longer. When I finally broke, I would've told them anything to make it stop."

"Demon cults are good at making people do what they want. A complete lack of morals combined with the ability to inflict unlimited pain make them master torturers." He didn't know why he was trying to reassure Timothy. The guy was a total stranger. Still, Daisuke felt the need to make the effort. "Don't be too hard on yourself."

Timothy let out a long sigh and threw his arm over his eyes. Somehow Daisuke doubted his words had done much good. There were councilors at the hospital that could hopefully help him. He set out again for the edge of the barrier.

He was burning daylight and the demons weren't going to imprison themselves.

When Vanessa finally appeared in the teleportation chamber of Castle Solomon, she let out a long sigh of relief. The sandstone walls had never looked so welcoming. Her time in Castle Ravenclaw's dungeon had left her tired and weak. Her magic had yet to recover. She was confident that it would eventually. She had to believe that or go mad.

Only access to a cache of supplies that included a teleportation stick had allowed her to safely return home. And she did think of this place as home, certainly more than the shabby apartment she'd lived in before joining the group.

She looked down at her filthy, wrinkled clothes. Best if she changed before reporting in to Lord Solomon.

The chamber door opened and a youth in a white robe stepped inside. The shapeless robe disguised the initiate's sex, but then a distinctly female voice said, "Lord Solomon sensed your arrival and asked that I escort you to the meeting room."

Vanessa grimaced. So much for changing her clothes. "Okay. Are any of the other members here?"

"No, ma'am. Everyone's out on missions. Only the initiates, the new chief archivist, the healers, and of course Lord Solomon are here at present."

Outside they turned right down the hall. Vanessa didn't need a guide, she knew every passage intimately, but she kept that to herself. The initiate was more of an honor guard than a guide. The three youngest members of the Blood of

Solomon handled all the menial labor in the castle while studying to make the most of their magic.

The room where she appeared was only a couple minutes away from the meeting room and soon her guide stopped and opened the door for her. "Welcome home, ma'am."

"It's good to be home." Vanessa smiled with genuine warmth and stepped inside.

At the head of the rectangular table, his tan robe smooth and crisp, and his white beard perfectly trimmed, sat Solomon the Great. The master of the order stood as she approached. "My poor sister. Look at the state of you. Our enemies will suffer greatly for this insult should they fall into our hands. How are you feeling?"

"Weak, my lord. And hollow without my magic. I humbly apologize for my many failures. I hope you can forgive me."

Lord Solomon guided her into the chair to his left then sat himself. "Dear Vanessa, none of us is perfect. Failing to see through Remi's lies was a failure on my part." She wanted to argue with him, but Lord Solomon kept talking. "All we can do is our best to bring the grand vision to reality. Now, tell me everything that happened."

She did so, making no effort to gloss over her many mistakes. When she finished, Lord Solomon appeared deep in thought, his eyes trained on the ceiling. At last he said, "The loss of three of Abaddon's demons is a blow, but more troubling to me is this mask-binding business. Demons are meant to be our servants, tools to bring about the great vision, not partners to bind with and corrupt our souls. I can't imagine what Remi is thinking."

"I'm sure the traitor has plans of his own," Vanessa said. "I can't imagine he left us only to serve as a demon priest's underling. I request permission to hunt him down once I'm fully recovered."

"Granted. It will also be useful to know the ultimate fate of Razak's prison. If our wayward brother hasn't claimed it, then we may yet do so."

Vanessa grimaced at the mention of Daisuke. "He's proving himself a greater pest than I expected."

"He is of the blood. After myself, he's probably the strongest of Solomon the Wise's descendants. That makes our failure to bring him into the fold all the more glaring."

She stared for a moment. Vanessa knew that Daisuke was strong, but strong enough to stand at Lord Solomon's right hand? She couldn't believe it.

"Don't worry about him for now," Lord Solomon said. "Rest, eat, and recover. The sooner you're ready to resume the hunt, the better."

She stood and bowed. "I won't fail you again."

Lord Solomon smiled. "Yes, you will. All of us will fail again. For all our power, for all the magic we command, we are still only human. And failure is a very human thing to do. Go on."

Vanessa took her leave. She didn't know just what to make of her lord's parting words, but she swore to herself that, at a minimum, she wouldn't fail to deal with Remi when next they met.

EPILOGUE

Daisuke wiped the sweat from his brow as he left the Circle's vault. Both demons had been returned to their respective prisons and were now safe and sound in storage. Neither demon put up anything close to the fight that Vorgon did. The trickiest part was separating Zog's essence from the mask. That binding had been impressive work. His respect for Remi's magical skills had gone up a couple of notches. The man himself was still a piece of trash, but his talent couldn't be denied.

Leaving the narrow passage that led to the vault, Daisuke took a deep breath of cool mountain air. That made four demons locked away and sixty-eight to go. When he thought about it that way, it was slightly depressing.

Ruq glided down and landed on his shoulder. His familiar didn't like going into the magic dead zone that housed the vault. Daisuke didn't especially like it either, but now that he knew where it was and had permission to enter, he figured there was no point in making the boss take a special trip out here.

"What now?" Ruq asked.

"Now we return to base, make our final report, and get something unhealthy for lunch. I suspect we'll be heading out again far sooner than we might prefer."

"What else is new?"

Daisuke grinned. Ruq certainly had a point.

Moving to the nearest shadow, Daisuke stepped through it and a moment later emerged in a special room in the shop. A rune circle covered the floor and only those that knew the secret of its magic could travel directly here.

He pushed the door open before the silver light of the runes faded and stepped into the hall. A short walk down familiar halls brought him to the boss's office. Before he could knock the door opened, revealing the boss in all her lovely splendor. As always she was dressed in an ash-gray suit. Her hair was combed back from her face and her lips were deep red. She smiled, her eyes glowing faintly as she did.

"You're done?"

"Yup, two demons in the vault. The computer didn't even threaten to shoot me."

"Of course not, that's the most advanced AI system in the world. It wouldn't make such a simple mistake. You'll be going after Razak next."

Daisuke nodded. "Figured. I've got the seal, so tracking down the prison shouldn't be too hard, assuming that Remi and the Devil Man don't have a hideout shielded against tracking magic."

"I'm more worried about what the Blood of Solomon are going to do. You just know Vanessa Warhawk has told her master what happened by now."

Daisuke shrugged. "I'll deal with them if and when I have to. How's Vixen?"

"Still unconscious. Rin doesn't think there's any permanent damage, but the trauma may have left her in shock." The boss gave a sad shake of her head. "The sorts of awful things one human will do to another never ceases to amaze me."

"Yeah, some members of the species aren't fantastic. If there's nothing else, I'm going to get some food and rest. I'll head back to Romania in the morning."

"Take Helena with you."

He frowned. "You sure? She's been through a lot. In some ways more than Jinx. I know her magic is back but still…"

"That's why she needs to go with you. She needs to be in the field to regain her confidence."

Daisuke had his doubts, but this wasn't an argument he was going to win. "If you say so, I'm happy for the company."

"I say so. And good luck."

"I'll take all I can get. Later, boss."

Daisuke left the office. Hopefully none of them would come to regret this decision. Time, as always, would tell.

AUTHOR NOTE

Hello there,

Thanks very much for checking out The Demon Masks. The adventure resumes in book 2 of this arc, The Hunt For The Devil Man. I hope you'll join me for the final confrontation between our heroes and Abaddon's Hellpriest.

Until next time,

James E. Wisher

Death Incarnate

Atlantis Rising

Rise of the Demon Lords

The Pale Princess

Malice

Hearts of Corrupt Fire

Aegis of Merlin Omnibus Vol 1.

Aegis of Merlin Omnibus Vol 2.

The Complete Aegis of Merlin Omnibus

The Immortal Apprentice Trilogy

The War With Audin (Prequel Novella)

The Hunt For Revenge

The Army of Darkness

The Apprentice Reborn

The Soul Bound Saga

An Unwelcome Journey

Darkness in Tiber

Depths of Betrayal

The Black Iron Empire

Overmage

The Divine Key Trilogy

Shadow Magic

For The Greater Good

The Divine Key Awakens

The Dragonspire Chronicles

The Black Egg

The Mysterious Coin

The Dragons' Graveyard

The Slave War

The Sunken Tower

The Dragon Empress

The Dragonspire Chronicles Omnibus Vol. 1

The Dragonspire Chronicles Omnibus Vol. 2

The Complete Dragonspire Chronicles Omnibus

Soul Force Saga

Disciples of the Horned One Trilogy:

Darkness Rising

Raging Sea and Trembling Earth

Harvest of Souls

Disciples of the Horned One Omnibus

Chains of the Fallen Arc:

Dreaming in the Dark

On Blackened Wings

Chains of the Fallen Omnibus

The Complete Soul Force Saga Omnibus

Other Fantasy Novels:

The Squire

Death and Honor Omnibus

The Rogue Star Series:

Children of Darkness

Children of the Void

Children of Junk

Rogue Star Omnibus Vol. 1

Children of the Black Ship

Children of The End

ABOUT THE AUTHOR

James E. Wisher is a writer of science fiction and Fantasy novels. He's been writing since high school and reading everything he could get his hands on for as long as he can remember.